RIVERBEND FRIENDS™

Real, Not Perfect
Searching for Normal
The Me You See
Chasing the Spotlight
Life in the Middle
Heart of Belonging

HEART OF BELONGING

Heart of Belonging

RIVERBEND FRIENDS™

C. J. Darlington

CREATED BY

Lissa Halls Johnson

A Focus on the Family resource
published by Tyndale House Publishers

29	28	27	26	25	24	23
7	6	5	4	3	2	1

For Vicki and Amy,
two dear friends who pulled me through.
Thank you from the bottom of my heart for loving
on me when I had nothing to give. Hope to have
you guys in my life for many years to come!

Chapter
1

I THOUGHT THAT FINDING OUT who my real father was would change my life. It did. Just not how I expected.

Mason King. My biological father. Knowing I shared blood with a famous horse trainer made me want to work with horses even more, if that were even possible. I had *always* been the crazy horse girl wearing cowboy boots and going to school smelling like a barn—long before I knew Mason King was my father. Now I might actually have a chance to be the horsewoman I'd always dreamed of. After all, I had it in my *genes*.

That has to mean something, right?

At least that's what I told myself when it was the middle of July and I was sweating like a pig while cleaning out horse stalls. I jammed the manure fork under a pile of fresh horse dung and sifted it from the pellet bedding lining the stall floor. The back of my T-shirt was already damp, and it was only eight in the morning. I grinned as I dumped the manure into the wheelbarrow outside the stall. Oh yeah. I was living the dream.

"Water break?"

Janie, the owner of Green Tree Farm—the barn where I'd been working for the past few months—appeared outside the stall, waving a bottle of Dasani water. The fifty-something woman always reminded me of a bulldog—short, stout, and harmless. She handed me the bottle, which must've come from her fridge. Condensation was building up on the plastic.

I eagerly unscrewed the cap and gulped down several icy swallows that almost made my throat cramp. "Thanks."

"Where's Sarah?" Janie asked.

"Didn't show," I said, setting the water bottle on the ground outside the stall and getting back to work. The horses should've been brought in a half hour ago, and I was going as fast as I could to get the stalls cleaned out. In summer, we turned the horses out overnight and brought them inside in the morning. And whoever did turnout last night should've cleaned out their stalls but hadn't.

"You did all this yourself?"

I nodded. Fourteen stalls. I was on the last one.

"Good work," Janie said.

I smiled. My boss could sometimes be gruff, like the bulldog she resembled, so I ate up any encouragement she offered, the way horses eat their grain.

"By the way, I believe your fan club is here," Janie said, chuckling. "I'll make my way back to the house."

"Shay!"

I startled at the exuberant greeting that came from across the barn and looked up to see three teen girls running toward us. I blinked. Tessa, Izzy, and Amelia were all smiles as they rushed over, loosing a cloud of excited energy through the barn.

"Hey, Shay!" Izzy giggled, her wild, curly hair bouncing a little. She was always amused at how that greeting rhymed.

I stepped out of the stall.

"Oh my gosh." Amelia groaned and stepped back, holding her nose. "You stink!"

"That's what you get for surprising me," I said with a huge smile of my own.

Tessa slipped her mirror aviator sunglasses onto the top of her head and patted my shoulder. "I'd give you a hug, but . . ." she said with a laugh, blatantly scanning me up and down. "I hope it was okay to stop in. I know how much you like surprises."

"You guys can surprise me any time."

"Whoa." Amelia raised her hands like she wanted me to back up. "Did I just hear Shay Mitchell say she is okay with surprises?"

"Only from you three." I grinned. "Don't press your luck." But she was right to find my reaction strange. I was usually the introverted girl who needed time to switch gears if plans changed, but these friends had caused that reluctant part of me to wither in a very good way. I was still shy, especially in unfamiliar situations, but I was more willing to try new things with them around. Being accepted for who you are can change you like that.

When I first moved to Riverbend to live with my aunt Laura above her indie bookstore, Booked Up, I was a shell of who I'd been before my adoptive dad died. Grief changes you too. I was continually amazed that these girls knew my biggest secret— a short stint I'd spent in juvie—and they still wanted to be friends. We were as different from each other as our fingerprints, but somehow we complemented each other so well, we were able to make a friendship work.

Tessa had such a kind and gentle manner. She stood firm in her convictions, yet she could be tripped up by her perfectionistic tendencies. She was harder on herself than anyone else, but she had been trying to work on that. Her organization and athleticism made her my go-to if I ever needed someone to help me make sense of my scattered thoughts or move a piece of furniture.

Amelia was probably the most spontaneous, dramatic, and

boisterous person I'd ever met. Fierce. She wouldn't let anyone tell her she couldn't or shouldn't do something. Watching her step boldly forward encouraged me to take risks, speak up, and think outside the box—at least once in a while.

Just thinking about Izzy made me laugh and get warm fuzzies inside. She'd made it her mission to "catch Shay up on the century" by introducing me to pop culture movies from the past and fun shows on Netflix. (Her favorite show is now mine. *Of course* it's about a girl who takes in horses with problems and by the end of the episode has diagnosed—and fixed—their problems.) And her love of animals, her cheerfulness, and her cupcakes were often exactly what I needed to bring me out of a darker mood.

Yeah, we were good for each other. I could only hope I brought something positive to each of them.

Then I got a whiff of my sweaty shirt. "Ugh, you're right. I do stink."

"Well," Amelia said, pointing at a blob on my jeans, "that might have something to do with it. Is that horse . . . poop?"

I didn't even have to look where she pointed. "Yep," I said.

"That would explain it." Amelia looked into the stall, which had brown piles of digested grass still waiting to be scooped. "Aren't you supposed to be done by now?"

I sighed. "Yeah."

"We'll help," Izzy said.

"You don't have to."

Izzy ignored me and grabbed a manure fork. Before I could protest any further, she was picking out the last few piles in the stall and laughing again. Her personality and the fact that she was a middle child sometimes allowed her to see humor in things that I, an only child, didn't. But Izzy's laughter was always contagious. It was all I could do to keep from cracking a grin.

I playfully smacked her arm. "Oh, stop."

Amelia reached hesitantly for the broom leaning against the stall, like it was contaminated with Covid. "Yep, we're helping you."

None of them were dressed for barn work in their shorts and tees, and Tessa and Izzy wore flip-flops. Izzy didn't seem to care. Tessa was more uncertain and seemed to be watching her step so her foot didn't land in something mushy.

Izzy grabbed the handles of the manure cart. "We're kidnapping you after we're done."

"Wait . . . what?" I said.

"Where's this go?" she asked without answering me.

I told her where the manure pile was located, and Izzy pushed the heavy cart toward the open barn door. The cart was filled to the top, and she was using all her body weight to get it going. Yet she didn't complain. Izzy couldn't have any pets because her brother was allergic, and anytime she got to be around animals, she was as happy as a duck in a rainstorm. If it were up to her, she'd probably have a house full of anything with four legs. Or even three legs. I sometimes joked that she probably wouldn't be friends with me if I didn't have a dog and cat.

"Ice cream!" Izzy suddenly shouted over her shoulder. "We're taking you to get ice cream."

I gave the other girls a quizzical look.

"A new ice cream shop just opened downtown," Tessa explained. "Mom and I went, and it's *uh-mazing*."

Amelia swept the aisle vigorously, stirring dust, hay, and who knew what else into the air. "How could you miss it, Shay? It's like a block from you."

Tessa and I watched Amelia's wild sweeping for a second until she noticed us staring and stopped. Tessa coughed. Amelia cocked her head like her Labradoodle sometimes did, and I lost it. It wasn't the first time my friend's gesture sent me into a laughing fit.

"What?" Amelia asked, clueless as usual about why we were amused. She touched her head. "Is it my hair?"

"No, no," I said. "Your hair is fine." Last year she'd rashly decided to chop off her beautiful long, curly, reddish hair into a pixie cut in an attempt to get the role of Peter in the musical *Peter Pan*. She'd regretted the decision almost immediately and was still self-conscious about how long it was taking to grow out.

"The head tilt," I said.

Amelia rolled her eyes. She'd heard this from me before.

"You do everything with such . . ." Tessa made a general motion with her hand. "Panache."

"Oh!" I said. "I have to bring the horses in!"

Izzy parked the empty cart and clapped her hands together. "Can I help?"

I pointed at her now-dusty flip-flops, shaking my head. It wasn't safe to be around horses in anything but boots, at least if you could help it. One accidental stomp, and Izzy's toes could be broken.

"Guys, my aunt needs me back at the store. I can't do ice cream."

"No, she doesn't," Tessa said.

Amelia started singing a crazy mishmash, made-up song about ice cream, wearing shoes around horses, and freedom from work. She sang like she was a rock star, and the broomstick became her microphone. The barn aisle was instantly transformed into her stage. But then, pretty much anywhere could be a stage for Amelia.

"We texted her," Tessa said.

"She said it was okay," Izzy agreed and began to dance to Amelia's song. My goodness, my friends could be silly. I wished I could just let go of my shyness and join in.

Tessa grabbed my shoulders from behind and pushed me toward the other open barn door, where the pastures were located. "Horses, Shay."

I jogged out to the first gate, where six geldings waited. The flies were already starting to bother the animals even though they wore fly masks, which were mesh coverings that went over their eyes and ears. Flies were merciless in the summer, especially in the day—another reason we turned the horses out at night from May to September.

As I led the horses in, my friends hung over the corral gates to watch. Izzy was completely unable to keep quiet and sounded like she was watching fireworks. "That one is so pretty. Wowww. That one's mane is beautiful!"

As Izzy *oohed* and *aahed*, I considered again what a gift it was to have friends teaching me to believe it was okay to just be me— Shay Mitchell, the crazy horse girl.

Chapter
2

By the time I brought in all but the last horse, I could feel more sweat dripping down my rib cage. I'd purposely saved the little gray mare, Ava, for last so I could take my time with her. Amelia and Izzy went back to sweeping the aisle, so only Tessa came out with me. We took a minute, just resting our arms on the metal gate, watching Ava graze. Her eye was on us, but she kept eating her grass as if knowing she needed to get in every bite she could before she had to go into her stall. Her dark tail swished from side to side, warding off flies.

"She's so pretty," Tessa said.

I had to agree. Ava was a dark gray color, with dapples and an almost black mane and tail, but her nose was white with pink skin. It made her look adorable and more like a pony. But even if she weren't beautiful, I'd still love her. She was the first horse I met here at Green Tree Farm, back when she'd been stuck in a stall because of a hoof abscess. She was also the horse I'd caught my biological father abusing at a horse clinic last fall.

"I still can't believe anyone would hurt her," I muttered. My friends had been at the clinic with me, so they knew the whole story. I'd been livid with the man at the time and swore I would never, ever be like him or even want to get to know him. But as the months passed, I'd found myself wondering about him again.

"Have you thought about contacting your father?" Tessa asked, as though reading my mind.

Ugh. Okay, I hadn't expected *that* question. I wasn't going to lie to her, but I wasn't sure if I wanted to answer her either.

My bio father was still out there, and he didn't know about me as far as I could tell. I'd started wondering nearly every day what he would think of me if he did. Would he even *want* a relationship with a kid he didn't know existed? Did *I* want one with *him*?

I turned toward Tessa. "Yeah, I've thought about it." Tessa understood these weird parental issues better than the others. After all, her dad had cheated on her mom and gotten the girlfriend pregnant. Just last week, Tessa had attended her father's wedding to that other woman, Rebecca. So she definitely knew about messy family dynamics.

"Makes sense that you want to," Tessa said. "Would also make sense if you didn't. He wasn't exactly a great guy from what you told me."

"Yeah," I said. "But what if that was a one-off and he isn't like that the rest of the time? Everyone has bad days and can lose control for a minute."

Tessa went quiet, her eyes on Ava. I got the feeling she was weighing how to respond, maybe because she understood how delicate the subject was.

"I know what he did," I added. "But I've messed up too."

She nodded. "That's not how you felt at the clinic, though."

"I've been thinking . . ." I said softly. "Maybe . . ." I couldn't tell her there were times I longed for a parent so badly that I was willing to fill the void with whatever.

Tessa gave me a kind, gentle look I could feel even though I couldn't see her eyes behind her sunglasses. "Just be safe," my friend said. "I don't want you to get hurt."

I went over and slipped a halter on Ava, then walked her through the gate. She willingly followed, and I gave her neck a gentle pat.

"Family can be complicated," Tessa said, matching my stride.

"No kidding. How are things with *your* dad?"

Tessa's flip-flops made a little flapping sound with each step she took. I thought about telling her she had a strand of hay in her hair but decided not to interrupt her thinking about my question.

"It's still hard," Tessa said. "But I want a relationship with my brother, and it seems like Rebecca and I have called a truce for now."

"And your mom's settling into the new house?"

"She loves it."

"You?"

Tessa smiled. "It's good. I miss our old house, but in a way it's nice to start over."

I kind of knew what she meant. After Dad died, if I'd had to keep living in the small house we'd been renting, it would've seemed weird. Everything, from the oil painting of the bucking bronc rider on the wall to the bathroom sink with the rusty drain where he shaved, would've reminded me of him. And even though Tessa's dad was still alive, it was probably a similar feeling. In fact, a part of her life *had* died when he'd left, and it had taken her the better part of a year to fully understand that. There was no going back. Only forward.

I needed to learn that too.

I walked Ava into the barn, and one of the other horses, a paint mare named Sky, nickered at her. She nickered back.

Izzy rested her broom against a stall door. "So . . . is Ava a horse or a pony?"

I led the mare into her stall, where I removed her halter and hung it on the hook beside the door. The little horse immediately started nibbling on the hay stuffed into her hay net hanging from the wall.

"Horse," I said. "Barely, though. She's 14.2 hands."

I closed only the bottom half of the Dutch doors of Ava's stall so she could poke her head out and be sociable if she wanted. Izzy hung over the door, probably hoping the mare would come to her. Amelia stayed a few feet back. She was a little more timid around the horses than I thought she would be.

"In English, Shay," Amelia said.

I smiled. Sometimes I forgot my friends didn't know a lot of horse lingo. They probably felt like I did when they flung around theater terms like *cyclorama* or *parodos*. "You measure how tall a horse is from the withers to the ground using 'hands.' A hand equals four inches, and ponies are usually under 14.2 hands. Over that is considered a horse."

"Withers?"

"Sorry!" I went into the stall again and touched Ava's neck above her shoulders at the base of her mane. "Withers are about here."

Izzy sighed. "I wish I knew as much about horses as you do." She was looking at Ava with the kind of longing gaze a puppy gives a meaty bone. Sometimes when we hung out at my place, my aunt's rescue greyhound, Stanley, would rest his head in Izzy's lap, and she would sigh with such contentment it made me sad she couldn't have a pet of her own.

I shrugged. "I don't know nearly as much as I want to." I'd taken a few lessons at a barn near my old house and done a lot of reading and watching horse training videos online, but the barn experiences I'd had in the past couple of months working here had been a crash course in a wider variety of horse knowledge.

"Well, you know way more than the three of us," Tessa said.

I almost blushed at the compliment. I wasn't good at receiving them, but I'd been trying to get better about that because my friends wouldn't say things they didn't mean.

"Good girl," I whispered to Ava, rubbing her gently on the shoulder. She turned her head in my direction and sniffed my arm. I hoped she understood I had tried my best to protect her from my bio father at that clinic. And I hoped she also knew I wasn't like him. Would it be betraying her if I talked to him someday?

"She loves you," Izzy said.

Her words warmed my heart even more. "I love her too."

"You should buy her!" Amelia said.

My friends crowded around the stall door, staring at me and Ava. The mare didn't seem to mind the attention as long as she was munching hay.

"I don't think I'll ever be able to afford a horse." I checked Ava's water bucket, which was full, and came out of the stall.

"How much do they cost?" Izzy asked.

Izzy's family might be able to buy one if they wanted. So could Amelia's, and even Tessa could save up and eventually buy, if not a horse, then some sort of pet. Her dad gave her money to babysit her little brother, and it was enough to help pay for a potential trip to Iceland someday with her mom. I was the poor one. Izzy had covered my lunch the last time we'd gone out together. I'd protested, but I was also thankful. I made a little spending money working shifts for my aunt, and Janie paid me for the work I did at the barn, but it wasn't much.

"Thousands," I answered. "The highly trained, specialized ones can be as much as or more than a new car."

"My stars!" Izzy said.

"And then you have to board them at a barn." I waved around at the horses safely tucked inside. Janie had bungee-corded fans to each of their stall bars, attempting to at least circulate the hot summer air—this was not a high-tech barn. "There's feed, and bedding, and hay, and vet bills." Lots of reasons why my aunt had told me I couldn't get a horse until I could pay for it myself.

"Are we done yet?" Amelia prodded, sweeping up the last of

the hay in the aisle. "Because ice cream is calling me." She placed the back of her hand on her forehead and tipped her head back in a gesture meant to make us smile. "I can hear its siren song."

My turn to roll my eyes at her antics. Sometimes Amelia was dramatic on purpose to be funny, but other times it was just her normal personality. I'm pretty sure this morning it was a little of both.

I made one last round to be sure all the stall doors were latched and the horses had full water buckets and hay nets. By the time I was done, even Izzy was getting impatient.

"Shay, come on!"

I wanted to explain to them that barns ran on a different schedule. If you intended to spend twenty minutes, it could morph into two hours in the blink of an eye. My aunt was used to my tardiness and had started telling me to text her when I was ready to be picked up because whenever I gave her a time, she ended up waiting in the car.

By nine thirty, we all piled into Tessa's Camry, me and Izzy in the back, and Amelia up front.

"Hope I don't smell up the car," I said.

"We still love you if you do." Tessa glanced at me in the rear-view mirror, and I smiled at her. For all our joking, I kinda needed to hear that.

I sank back into my seat and waited for the A/C to start working, surrounded by friends who cared about me enough to surprise me with a spontaneous ice cream excursion. It felt pretty good. Even if I was a sweaty mess. "I've missed you guys," I said softly. I wasn't one to always speak up and share what I was feeling, especially sentimental stuff, but I wanted them to know I appreciated them. I mean, how often did I tell them?

"Same!" Izzy said with a huge sigh.

"I thought we were going to hang out more this summer," I said.

"Yeah, me too," Tessa agreed.

We'd all been busier than we'd expected. Besides babysitting her little brother, Tessa kept long hours at the pool attending swim team practices and giving kids swimming lessons. Summer theater consumed most of Amelia's free time. Izzy and I had hung out some, but she'd recently been on a kick to try every single hobby under the sun. As for me, between my work at the bookstore and my responsibilities at the barn, I was as tied down as any of them. I hadn't even been able to go to Tessa's dad's wedding because of an important author reading/book signing event I had to help my aunt with. I guess that made these moments together extra special. I exhaled and took it all in. I wasn't going to ruin the chance at some quality time with my friends.

As Tessa drove down the narrow dirt lane that led to the road, a big black pickup truck came toward us, and Tessa had to drive almost into the grass so it could pass.

"Who's that?" Amelia asked.

I was craning to see the driver through the dust cloud. "Have no idea."

"They own one of the horses?"

I was pretty sure I was familiar with all the boarders, and the farm wasn't open to drop-ins, but that didn't mean it never happened. The reason I was even here working at the barn was that one day last fall I'd stopped in to visit the horses and met Janie, who happened to be looking for barn help. But for some reason, an uneasy feeling crept over me at the sight of that truck, and I struggled to keep my cheerful mood. We pulled out onto the main road, and I lost sight of the vehicle, but the unease was harder to lose.

Chapter
3

"I DON'T BELIEVE IT." Amelia crossed her arms, staring up at the brand-new ice cream parlor. A decorative, gold-painted ice cream cone beckoned from the front window underneath the business name, The Sweet Spot. I peered inside and saw red padded stools lined up at a retro red-laminate counter. The freezer case was empty, and not a soul was in sight.

Tessa read the hours from a small schedule next to the door. "They don't open 'til noon."

"But their website said nine!" Amelia wailed.

"On Saturdays," Tessa said, pointing at the proof.

Amelia stomped her foot. "I *know* I didn't read it wrong."

Izzy rested her hand on Amelia's shoulder. "Maybe they changed it?"

"What are we going to do?"

The way Amelia sounded, this was the crime of the century. I loved how deeply she felt things and how passionate she could be if she determined a cause was worth fighting for. She's part of the reason I'd survived my audition for the school play last year without passing out. She had believed in me—or at least done a darn good job pretending she did—even though, let's face it, drama class and I hadn't exactly been friends from the get-go. I was so glad I wasn't taking it again this year. For me, the only good thing about it was that I'd met these girls.

"It's okay," I said, trying to hide my own disappointment.

"No, it's not!"

I couldn't tell if my friend was hangry or if there was something else bothering her.

"How long has it been since we did something *together*?" Amelia asked, her cheeks reddening in the morning sun. "It would've been perfect."

"Grounds and Rounds is open," Izzy, forever the peacemaker, suggested. That was our favorite coffee shop and where we often met up, but it felt like that's what we always did if we weren't hanging out in "our" alcove in the bookstore. I was with Amelia—up for trying something different.

"Come on, Amelia." Izzy looped her arm around Amelia's, gently pulling her toward the coffee shop. "You can sue the ice cream parlor later."

I snorted.

"Oh my gosh!" Amelia stopped in her tracks like a horse who caught sight of the trailer it was about to be loaded on. She planted her feet and wouldn't move.

Tessa threw her hands up. "Now what?"

"I can't find my phone!"

"And we're surprised because . . ." Tessa said.

Amelia's face was getting redder by the second. "What if I can't find it? What am I going to tell my parents? This would be the second phone I've lost this year."

"I'm sure you'll find it," I said. "You always do. Where'd you have it last?"

"I don't remember!"

Tessa held up her keys. "I'll check the car." A minute later, she came back empty-handed. "Sorry, not there."

"Did you have it at the barn?" Izzy asked.

"I . . . yes." Amelia nodded vigorously. "I took a selfie with that gray pony." Then her eyes widened. "What if a horse *steps* on it?" She covered her face with her hands.

"Did you take a photo of me?" Izzy asked, her voice sounding almost panicked.

"What?" Amelia said.

"Of me, a photo of me," Izzy repeated.

"I don't remember."

"Can you please delete it if you did?"

Amelia gave Izzy a stare down. "Why?"

"Please. It's important."

"Guys," I said. "Focus. Amelia, did you set your phone down?"

"I can't remember!"

"Try," I said, and Amelia glared at me.

Her look kind of surprised me. It wasn't exactly unusual for her to misplace her cell. We'd all come to accept it as a part of who she was—Amelia, the girl who misplaced things.

She grabbed her head and closed her eyes.

I gave Tessa a questioning look. She shrugged.

Amelia's eyes flew open. "Yes!"

"Yes what?" Izzy said.

"I set it on a hay bale."

Okay, that was good. Maybe. "Where was the bale?" I asked.

"We have to go back." Amelia ran for Tessa's Camry, the tail of her loose, multicolored peasant shirt flowing behind her.

"Hey, wait up," Izzy said, somehow managing to run in her

flip-flops. Tessa and I took longer, and the other two girls were already in the car and buckled by the time we got there.

"Hurry, before it's too late!" Amelia exclaimed. "We're on a mission!"

I tried not to be irritated that I wasn't going to be eating ice cream or sipping something with caffeine anytime soon. There would be no peace until that phone was found.

The drive back to the barn was only a few minutes, but it felt a lot longer because Amelia and Izzy started their "Name That Musical" game, something I majorly stunk at. The only musical I knew much about was *The Sound of Music*, and my knowledge of that was limited to a couple of songs and the name of the lead actress in the movie.

"Have you seen the movie version of *Dear Evan Hansen* yet?" Izzy asked, and I realized the question was for me.

"Uh . . ."

She pulled out her phone. "I'll add it to the list." Dad and I didn't watch much TV, but I hadn't realized I was so sheltered until meeting these girls.

Tessa turned onto Green Tree Farm Lane, her car kicking up dust until she parked in the small gravel lot. We climbed out, and Amelia started to run through the open doors at the end of the barn but quickly stopped and power walked instead. I'd yelled at her for running around horses before, and apparently, she remembered. Some horses could spook at their own shadow. We didn't need to give them any other excuses.

I followed my friends into the barn, but not before I noticed that the black truck had parked close to Janie's house. My mind whirled like Amelia's dust tornado with all kinds of catastrophic thoughts. Why did my mind always catapult toward the worst-case scenario? Couldn't the poor woman have company over without throwing me into a panic?

I turned away and stepped into the barn. "Did you find it?"

My friends were all standing outside Ava's stall. The mare hung her head over the door, craning to say hello to Amelia's shirt. But my friend didn't notice and remained just out of reach. "Oh my gosh, it's gone forever!" she said, looking frantically around her personal bubble.

"No, it's not," I said.

"You don't know that," she snapped.

Well, true, but what were the chances it wasn't somewhere around here? I decided not to suggest it had fallen out of her pocket and landed in the wheelbarrow full of manure.

Tessa pulled out her own phone. "I'll call it."

Amelia clasped her hands together like she was praying. "Oh, yes. Please, please, please." She closed her eyes again and seemed to be murmuring something as we all waited to hear "Defying Gravity"—her current ringtone.

When we heard some faint singing, all four of us went on alert.

"Where's it coming from?" Izzy asked.

I could hear a voice hitting a high note. I peered inside Ava's stall. Nothing there. The sound got louder and seemed to be coming from the aisle.

Izzy dropped to her hands and knees by Sky's stall. "I got it!" She popped up and waved the phone.

Amelia rushed over to her, took the phone, kissed it, and clasped it to her chest. "Thank you, Izzy, my phone rescuer!"

Izzy put up both her palms. "I don't need a thank-you kiss, though."

We all laughed.

"Try to keep it with you," I said, then threw Tessa a look. She was already throwing one exactly like it back at me. Without a word and with a hint of a smile, we conveyed the truth that we'd probably be helping Amelia on another rescue mission sometime in the not-too-distant future. Even though we might complain sometimes, we felt that her forgetfulness, while annoying, was also endearing and a part of who she was. When you care for someone, you have to take the whole package, not just the good parts.

"Now can we please go and get some coffee?" I asked.

Tessa elbowed me. "Since when do you drink coffee?"

"Since I started working here." I gestured toward the horses and barn. I'd been getting up at five every day, and sometimes by noon I was ready to fall back into bed. I gave Ava a parting scratch on the neck. "See you tomorrow, girl."

"Let's blow this popsicle joint!" Amelia said, pumping her fist into the air.

All of us turned to leave just as Janie, along with a man and woman I didn't recognize, walked into the barn. Janie looked at us like we were a group of juvenile foxes caught in the chicken house. "What are you doing here?" she asked. Her tone was uncharacteristically sharp, and it set me immediately on edge.

I found myself stammering. "Uh . . . we forgot . . ."

Amelia held up her cell. "My phone. I accidentally dropped it over there by the hay."

I glanced at the couple with Janie. They were both probably in their midfifties, and the guy had a few days' worth of beard growth. A small embroidered horse galloped across the woman's blue polo shirt. Her graying hair was done up in a messy bun, and when she smiled at me, crow's-feet popped up around her eyes.

"Hello," she said, and I waited for Janie to introduce them.

But the moment turned into several uncomfortable seconds as Janie stood there with this weird, emotionless expression on her face. I wanted to get out of there as quickly as I could. Obviously, something was going on. Who *were* these people? Why didn't Janie want us there?

"We . . . we're on our way out," I stammered.

I started toward the door, but the woman stepped closer and stuck out her hand. "I'm Denise," she said. "This is my husband, Brad."

I shook it. Her grip was firm. So was his.

"Um, I'm Shay. These are my friends Izzy, Amelia, and Tessa."

"Nice to meet you," Denise said, shaking hands with each girl, her husband following suit.

Janie cleared her throat, finally finding her voice. "Shay cleans stalls for me and helps out with the horses in other ways."

"Oh, you do?" Brad grinned. "No shortage of *work* when it involves horses, eh?"

Were these people Janie's friends, her family, or potential boarders? I couldn't figure it out as none of those options made sense. Janie had never mentioned family, and I'd never seen friends of hers here. And only once in a blue moon would a client move and create a stall opening.

"Are you bringing a horse?" I asked.

"We're considering it," Brad said. "We have ten of them."

"Ten?" I felt a flash of panic at the ramifications of so many new horses arriving. That meant many of my horse friends had to be leaving. It was the only way there would be room for the new boarders. I looked over at Janie, hoping she would explain, but she glanced away.

"We really like what we see," Denise said. "This barn could be exactly what we've been looking for."

Now I was thoroughly confused. My heart started tapping against my rib cage.

"I'm sorry?"

Janie still wouldn't look at me.

My friends had gone silent, and the air felt oppressive from more than the summer heat as I tried to make sense of everything no one was saying.

Finally, Janie stepped toward me, her shoulders slumped. "I didn't tell you because it wasn't final yet."

"Oh, I'm sorry," Denise said. "I thought . . ."

"Tell me what?" My throat went tight, like it did before I cried.

Janie sighed and wouldn't look at me, staring at her dusty boots. That gave it away. It wasn't good news. No one about to tell you something good beats around the bush.

"Shay, I'm selling the farm."

Chapter
4

"OKAY, SO HERE'S WHAT WE'RE GOING TO DO." Izzy sat next to me in the back seat of Tessa's car as we pulled away from the farm.

I was still in shock. How long had Janie known? When was she planning to tell me? Was it definite? When was it happening? But the biggest question that gripped me like a police dog's jaws on a criminal's leg was . . . *what was going to happen to the horses?*

I tried to snap myself back into the present and focus on Izzy.

"Take us to the grocery store," Izzy called up to Tessa.

"What?" Tessa eyed Izzy in the rearview. I imagined her eyebrows rising in a perplexed expression under her sunglasses. "Why?"

"I'm okay," I whispered to Izzy.

"Not so sure about that," she responded.

Amelia turned around in her seat. "Why are we going to the grocery store?"

Izzy wrapped her arm around my shoulders and squeezed me

hard in her attempt at a sideways hug—while both of us wore seat belts. Izzy would often hug me for no reason, practically crushing my ribs, but that was her way with everyone.

"I'm making you all lunch," Izzy said. "And we're going back to Shay's house because I'm making Stanley a sandwich too."

I didn't have the energy to protest her offer, and I appreciated that she was taking charge. My aunt wouldn't mind. She was always encouraging me to invite my friends over.

An hour later, we'd all gathered in my aunt's small kitchen with two bags of groceries unpacked on the counter and Izzy busy at the stove. The kitchen was her element. It didn't matter if she was baking fancy cupcakes—her specialty—or grilling cheese sandwiches like she was doing for us now; strap an apron on that girl and she became a force.

"Are you sure you don't want help?" I asked. I felt useless sitting at the table with the other girls, watching Izzy cook, but she was all smiles. She'd slipped on a headband to hold back her curls, and she waved the metal spatula at me.

"Sit and relax. I've got this!"

And she did. These weren't simple grilled cheese sandwiches. Izzy had bought fresh tomatoes and basil, onions to caramelize, and a block of mozzarella cheese.

Stanley, my aunt's brindle greyhound, sat on his haunches and watched Izzy's every move at the stove, waiting for something to drop onto the floor. He took his job cleaning the kitchen floor very seriously. He'd already snagged a piece of whole grain bread I was pretty sure Izzy had purposely let fall.

"What are you thinking?" Tessa asked me.

I let out a long sigh, taking a sip of one of the iced hazelnut coffees Tessa had bought for me and her at the grocery store. Izzy had gotten a root beer, and Amelia now nursed a bottle of forbidden Dr Pepper.

"She should've told you," Amelia said with a huff. She'd been ready to give Janie a piece of her mind right then and there at the barn, but thankfully, she'd held back. I didn't want to make the already bad situation worse, but I'd never seen Janie so guarded. She'd acted less tough bulldog and more worried Chihuahua.

I smiled at my friend's protectiveness. All three of them had closed ranks around me.

"It's her farm," I said, gripping my glass with both hands.

"So that couple might buy the place?" Amelia said.

I shrugged. "It looks that way."

"They seemed nice," Izzy offered, flipping the first of the grilled cheese sandwiches.

"I don't care if they're Mother Teresa and Saint Francis of Assisi. It still feels like the rug's been yanked out from under me."

Tessa cracked a smile. I supposed it was good I still had a trace of humor left. "I mean, I wonder why she's selling," I said. "I thought she was going to start a lesson program."

"That place has got to be worth a lot," Amelia said, running her fingers through her curls. Her phone sat on the table in front of her, and I almost reminded her to put it in her pocket or purse so she wouldn't forget it again.

"We don't need to talk about this," I said.

"Um, hello?" Amelia took a big gulp of Dr Pepper. "This is big, Shay. And it matters to you, so it matters to us."

"Thanks," I said. "I *just* started to get into the swing of the barn work, and now it's gone."

"Maybe it won't happen for a while," Tessa said.

"Your house sold in a week," I reminded her.

"Yeah, but a farm is different."

I wanted to believe that, but as Amelia had pointed out, Green Tree was prime real estate, and Janie had kept it up. It wasn't some run-down facility that would require tens of thousands of dollars to fix up. It was a turnkey property. If only Aunt Laura had more money and didn't already own a book business, I'd beg her to buy it.

"Who wants the first one?" Izzy held up a plate.

Stanley jumped to his feet, staring at the steaming sandwich while licking his chops.

"Yours is coming," Izzy told him. She placed the plate in front of me. "Let's pray quick so you can eat it while it's hot." She grabbed one of my hands, and Tessa reached for the other. We made a small circle around the table.

"Father, we ask You to help Shay make sense of everything," Izzy said. "Give her peace and comfort. We ask that You bless this food and that it would bring health to our bodies. Amen."

"Amen," I said, the others echoing.

"Hey." Tessa nudged me with her arm. "It'll work out."

She was trying to help, but optimism wasn't what I wanted, even though it might be what I needed. I wanted less "God has everything under control" and more "Man, that sucks, Shay." Or better yet, "We'll buy the farm for you."

"I hope it falls through," I said. I took a bite of the sandwich and chewed. *Oh, wow.* Hard to stay in the doldrums when eating something that tasty. The melted cheese and tomato flavors burst in my mouth. "This is delicious."

Izzy beamed. She gave her spatula a little victory shake. "One of my specialties."

"We need to pray for God's will to be done regardless," Amelia said.

That would not be easy for me—to pray or to believe. I felt like I was the least spiritual of my friends. All three of them were much better Christians than I was. They were the ones who went to church regularly. They were the ones who could spout a perfect Bible verse when needed. They were almost always the ones initiating prayer about something. Izzy had tried to get all of us to join her in a read-the-Bible-in-a-year challenge, but I had dragged my feet to commit. It wasn't that I didn't think it was important. I knew reading the Bible was good and valuable, and it would be easier to do if there was a schedule to follow. It was more that I knew I'd fall behind and disappoint not only her but also myself. Why commit to something that would end in failure?

A hammer of guilt hit me when I realized I hadn't logged into the Bible app on my phone in at least a week, probably two. Worse, I had a physical Bible somewhere in my room, but I had no idea where.

Dad and I hadn't gone to church with any kind of regularity, but it didn't mean we didn't love God or weren't Christians. I'd asked Jesus into my heart when I was a little girl. Not long after moving to Riverbend, I'd started going to church with Tessa and her mom whenever I didn't have a shift at the barn, but I got the feeling that was less often than they thought I should be going.

Yep. I was a big failure in the Christian department.

"In all honesty, I don't want to pray about it," I muttered.

By the looks on my friends' faces, I should've kept that to myself.

"But prayer works!" Izzy exclaimed.

Yeah, right, I wanted to say. *Did prayer keep Tessa's family together? What about protecting my dad or keeping my mom alive?* My thoughts continually ran the old *If God is good, why do bad things happen?* question everyone thinks about but few Christians voice. Nonbelievers didn't hesitate to blurt that one out.

"It's fine. I'll figure it out," I said, trying to smile and rein in my thoughts that were turning melancholy quicker than I could stop them. I took another bite of my grilled cheese and made an appreciative sound so Izzy would know how tasty it was. "Thanks for making this, Izzy."

I wasn't sure how long it would take me to process that Green Tree Farm might not be in my future like I'd hoped—like I needed—but I had to put it off until later, when my friends weren't around.

—m—

That afternoon, I told Aunt Laura about the farm as I handed her the extra sandwich Izzy had made for her. My aunt set it on the counter and focused on me. She was a thirty-something entrepreneur with a full life who'd given me a chance when no one else had. That couldn't have been easy. She still worked in her bookstore for an insane number of hours, but when your store and your apartment are in the same building, you can get more creative on how to spend time with your niece. Sometimes we'd watch Netflix on her tablet at the counter in between helping customers.

"Wow, Shay. That stinks."

"It's okay," I said, even though it wasn't.

Aunt Laura tucked her wavy dark hair behind her ears and brought out her laptop. To satisfy both our curiosities, she quickly went online to see if she could find a real estate listing for the farm. No such luck.

"Maybe it's a private sale," she said, tapping at her laptop.

I slumped into the sofa and groaned.

"You're not okay, kiddo."

"No," I mumbled.

"I'm sorry. Maybe the new owners will be even better?"

I groaned again in my best teen-girl tone. My phone vibrated in my pocket, and I pulled it out.

Text from Tessa. **How are you?**

Me: **Been better.**

Tessa: **I hear you.**

Me: **Didn't expect this.**

Tessa: **It's the surprising things that hit the hardest.**

Me: **Yeah.**

Come on, Shay, you can say more here. This is your friend. She's been there for you. I stared at my phone screen. Why did I find it so difficult to be vulnerable with people—even with someone like Tessa?

Aunt Laura came over and gave my shoulder a pat. "It's gonna work out," she said. It felt better coming from her than from my friends, but adults said that sort of stuff all the time and things still turned out awful. At least she didn't add "I promise." I really hated when people promised things they had zero control over. I'd even been known to yell at characters on TV when they said such nonsense.

Not knowing how to respond to Aunt Laura, I mumbled something unintelligible. Being so tired didn't help things.

"Sorry to tell you this now, but your grandmother wants to pick you up tomorrow."

That got my attention.

I jerked my head up. "Does she have to?"

Aunt Laura gave me the "mom" look she was perfecting way too well.

"Why is she picking me up?" I asked. "I'd rather you did."

"That's flattering," Aunt Laura said. "But I think you need to let her. She mentioned taking you out to eat or something."

Stanley came over and rested his head in my lap.

"See, even Stanley thinks so," Aunt Laura said.

As much as I wanted to, I had no right to complain too much about it. My grandmother was part of the reason Stanley even had his leg. She'd anonymously paid for the emergency surgery to save it after he got hit by a car. I never would have known except Aunt Laura wanted me to see that Grams really did care about me—at least a little.

I rested my hand on Stanley's head, stroking his ears. Fine. Maybe spending a little time with my grandmother wouldn't be as bad as I thought.

Chapter

5

THE NEXT MORNING, I rushed to get my barn work done early, both to beat the Indiana heat and because Grams was usually punctual and didn't like to wait. The other barn worker, Sarah, had gone MIA again, so I tried to focus on my chores and not on the fact that I had no idea if I'd be working here much longer. Definitely easier said than done. I nearly cried when I brought Ava in. It was too distressing to think about not seeing this sweet mare nearly every day. Janie was nowhere to be found, and I figured that was a good thing. What would I say to her without becoming a soppy mess?

By the time I finished, I was stinky and sweaty again. I slapped the fabric of my jeans with my palms, trying to dust off the dirt. At nine o'clock, I opened the passenger door to my grandmother's running SUV and relished the blasting A/C.

"Is that what you're wearing?"

I ducked down to see my grandmother, the most put-together-looking woman I knew. Today she even wore a strand of pearls over her pink, crisp, sleeveless blouse. A faint whiff of perfume hit my nose.

"Um, yeah?"

I took in my grandmother's pinched expression, sensing a lecture coming.

"Didn't you bring a change of clothes?"

I climbed into the car. The thought hadn't crossed my mind. Most days, I finished my work at the barn and Aunt Laura picked me up. She never seemed to mind if I smelled like a barn or if a few chunks of dirt rolled around on her floorboards. Tessa, Izzy, and Amelia hadn't minded either.

Grams sighed and backed out of the parking space. "I am never going to understand you."

Her tone wasn't mean, but it still stung. I could feel my heart pumping a little faster than normal, and I tried to breathe like I'd learned from that article online about calming down. Deep breath in, long breath out. It helped a little.

"I usually change when I get home," I said softly.

"Shay, we're eating in a restaurant."

I glanced down at my hands. That was probably a manure stain on my finger, and the dirt under my nails was going to take some scrubbing to come clean. I should have washed them in the utility sink, or at the very least hosed them off. "Aren't we going to Grounds and Rounds?" No one had ever stared at me in there, even when I'd come straight from the barn.

"I *was* planning something a little fancier," Grams said.

"We can still—"

"Grounds and Rounds will have to work."

"If you drop me off at the bookstore first, I can clean up."

My grandmother turned onto the road. "We'll go to the coffee shop."

Breathe in, breathe out.

This is the way it always seemed to go with my grandmother

and me. Some days, I could see she was trying to connect with me—like when she'd paid for Stanley's surgery. But other days, I wondered if the woman *liked* me at all. Even a smidge.

"So . . . how are things, Grams?"

Ugh. *What a dumb way to start a conversation.* I wanted to face-palm. What a dork I could be sometimes.

"Your grandfather and I will be leaving for the cottage next week."

"That'll be fun," I said.

"We were hoping you would come with us."

Here it was. The real reason she was taking me to breakfast. And, knowing Grams, this wasn't a subject she would simply let go of. I couldn't figure out why she would want me, a teenager she didn't understand, to go with them anyway. I suspected it had more to do with me choosing them over anything else in my life.

"Grams, I can't. Not this year."

"Can't or won't?"

I tried to remind myself it was a good thing she wanted me to spend time with her—even if I didn't understand why. Wasn't that a step up from dropping me off at my aunt's without saying goodbye like she had last fall? I'd been a huge disappointment to her then, and it felt like I still was now. Occasionally she'd throw out these little morsels of grandmotherly attention that confused me more than anything. Which was it? Was I the granddaughter she could be proud of, or the one she inherited like a hand-me-down who wasn't even related to her by blood?

"I've made some friends," I said.

"I know. That's very good."

"And I want to hang out with them."

"You have the entire year to hang out with your friends, Shay." Grams held the steering wheel tightly, and I noticed the ring with the huge ruby she always wore. Apparently, my adoptive dad, her son Greg, had given it to her for her fiftieth birthday.

"That's different," I said.

"Do you not want to spend time with your family?"

I stared down at my hands again. I didn't wear rings because it wasn't safe when working with horses. Janie told me a story about a woman whose ring got caught on a horse's shoe while she was picking its feet, and she ended up losing her finger.

"It's a valid question, Shay."

"Why do you do this?" I nearly whispered.

"I'm just asking a question."

I didn't have to look at my grandmother to imagine her shaking her head. *Here we go again. Shay, the disappointment of a granddaughter, letting her family down.*

Chapter
6

By the time we got to Grounds and Rounds, my stomach was growling, but I wasn't sure if I'd be able to eat. Though maybe a grilled cheese sandwich would match the grilling I suspected my grandmother had planned for me. After Izzy's masterful grilled cheese yesterday, anything else would seem like a plain bologna-on-white-bread sandwich.

I wished Tessa, Izzy, or Amelia were here with me instead of Grams. I pulled my phone from my back pocket and zapped out a text on our group thread.

Me: @ Grounds & Rounds w/ Grams. Wish u were here!

I stared at my screen, waiting for a response. But my friends were silent.

"It's rude to text when you're in the company of other people," Grams whispered to me as we walked to the counter to order.

That's when I saw the two girls at the table in the corner. I hoped they wouldn't notice me. Jade and Kelsey from school had bullied me last fall, and even though that was behind us and they'd left me alone the rest of the school year, I knew what they were made of. They were giggling over something on Jade's phone. Kelsey, who looked like a Scottish princess, swung her gorgeous auburn hair out of her face. Jade was model worthy. She was the type who could walk an international stage as Miss America or Miss World or Miss Wherever.

I focused on the chalked menu on the wall, trying to concentrate on what I might be able to eat. I ended up choosing a sausage-and-cheese bagel sandwich and a vanilla latte. Grams got coffee and an egg white omelet with spinach and feta.

I guided us to a table far away from the older girls, but Grams didn't want to sit near the window since the sun would shine in our faces. The only other free table was right next to Jade and Kelsey.

Breathe, Shay. Breathe.

I sat with my back to the girls, but not before Jade gave me a little finger wave. I forced myself to wave back. Hopefully they'd be so engrossed in their phones, they wouldn't hear me and Grams. My phone vibrated. I didn't dare check it with my grandmother's eyes on me.

The wait for our food seemed to stretch on and on, like the intermission of that old *Ten Commandments* movie Izzy had made me watch at the classics movie theater during spring break. I sipped on my latte. Sounds of coffee beans in the grinder, the slam-bang of the filter basket being emptied, mugs clinking together, and milk being frothed flowed around us like the foam swirled in my drink.

"I'm glad we're doing this," my grandmother said in a surprisingly happy tone.

And I had thought she was mad at me.

"Um, doing what?"

"This." She waved around, indicating the coffee shop. "Having breakfast. Talking. It's beneficial for us."

To me, it felt as beneficial as stubbing my toe, but I nodded. My grandmother wasn't a bad person, but I didn't think she realized how sharp her words could cut. Lately, it seemed like every conversation we shared forced me to sift through the meanings to try to figure out what she really wanted. There always seemed to be subtext, an agenda. It was never a plain "Hey, Shay, let's hang out and shop" or "Tell me about your day." She always wanted something from me that I wasn't able to quite get a handle on. On the rare occasions I understood what she wanted, I couldn't seem to give it to her. And I would never bring up the subject of my bio dad, something that was important to me but upsetting to my grandmother.

Jade and Kelsey laughed loudly behind me. I was half tempted to spin around and join them. Talking with my former enemies felt easier than talking with Grams.

"Why do you want me to go to the cottage with you?" I asked.

Grams chuckled. "That's a ridiculous question."

Was it? My grandmother made it perfectly clear last fall that she couldn't deal with my "behavior." I'm thankful now that I'd been dumped on Aunt Laura. Living with my aunt had become easier as time passed. We'd fallen into a simple routine, and I'd started to think we were actually good for each other. My aunt seemed to appreciate not being alone all the time, and I hoped that spending time with my mom's younger sister would bring me closer to understanding what Mom had been like.

A girl with pink hair who'd been behind the counter earlier brought our food to us. The food was a good distraction. I took a big bite of my bagel.

"It could be extremely valuable for you," Grams said, daintily cutting her omelet with her fork and a knife.

Who cuts eggs with a knife?

"You need to get beyond the limits of this town and explore all that life has to offer."

"But I'm happy here."

Grams laughed. "So is the caged bird that has never flown."

"Dad and I went to a lot of places, Grams." I took another bite of my bagel and nearly scalded my tongue on the sausage. "And I've even thought about visiting Mason King's ranch someday."

I swallowed my food and felt it slide all the way down my throat. Felt like it burned my esophagus along the way. I shouldn't have said that. My grandmother was obviously aware that I'd found out who my bio father was and that I had gone to see him at a clinic last year. She'd probably assumed my curiosity had been satisfied since I hadn't brought him up again. I should've let it stay that way.

Grams set down her fork, and it hit the plate sharply. "Are you planning on spending the summer with *him*?"

"Grams, he doesn't even know I exist."

There was that pinched expression again, like my grandmother had taken a bite out of a lemon.

"I was curious. I wanted to see him, and I did," I said. "I've only thought about visiting him again, but I doubt I will."

"What would your father think about all this?"

This was turning ugly fast. My phone vibrated again, and this time I pulled it out.

Two texts from my friends.

Tessa: How's it going?

Izzy: Wish we were there too!☺

I quickly tapped out a response, wishing I had time to think of a better one.

Me: Uh, not good.

I set my phone on the table faceup so I could see any texts as they came in. It would make me feel less alone. My friends could be here in spirit through the screen.

I looked up to see my grandmother staring pointedly at the phone and then glaring at me. "Really, Shay. It can't wait?"

"Sorry," I muttered. Taking in another deep breath, I tried to calm myself.

"I didn't want Greg to marry your mother." Grams cut two more slices from her omelet. "But he insisted he was madly in love. If he'd only listened to me, he might have spared himself, and you, so much heartache."

Okay, that cut deep.

"I told him of my suspicions," Grams continued, looking off into the distance, almost as if I wasn't there. "I tried to warn him."

Jade and Kelsey had gone silent behind me, and I wondered if they were listening to my grandmother. I couldn't say I'd blame them. She was creating more drama than the One Act we did for school. Everything in me wanted to shout at her to *stop*, but as always, the word stayed locked inside.

My phone's screen lit up.

Amelia: Oh no!! What's happening?

I reached for it, but my grandmother was faster. She dropped her hand over the screen and slid the phone to her side of the table, that ruby ring practically pulsing with the intensity I felt from her.

"We are having a discussion," Grams said. "You do not need to be on this thing." She flipped the phone over.

Deep breaths weren't helping anymore. "Do we have to talk about Mom? Can't we talk about something else?" I squeaked out. *What* we would talk about, I had no idea.

Grams sighed. "Honesty is so important, Shay. I want to be honest with you just as I want you to be with me. That's real communication."

"I *am* being honest. I told you I don't want to go to the cottage. I want to stay here for the summer with my friends and work at the barn." I stopped short. *If* there was going to be a barn in my summer.

My grandmother fixed her intense gray-blue eyes on me. I used to imagine myself growing up and looking like her. I wanted to have her poise, a refined sense of who I was. But staring into Grams's eyes, I was reminded I would never look anything like her. Be anything like her. As much as my adoptive father loved me, our genes were completely different, and I wouldn't carry a single one. It never used to matter to me, but it seemed to matter to my grandmother. I thought love was thicker than blood. That was Dad's mantra, but now I was beginning to doubt the truth of it. Grams said we were family, yet she'd once implied in an argument with my aunt that I wasn't really her granddaughter—biologically at least. And although Grams said she wanted to have me in her life and invited me to their cottage, she was the one who had sent me away to live with my aunt.

"Don't you think your father would be hurt if he knew you'd sought out this . . . this . . . sperm donor?"

I always thought it was unfair when she asked me questions like this. I wasn't a quick thinker. It took me time to respond because I processed things slowly—and processed best when I was alone. And goodness! I had no idea what my dad would think of my life now. I supposed I had let him down in some ways, but wouldn't he be proud that I was following my heart? He had always encouraged my love of horses. And that love of horses was, quite possibly, genetic.

"This *sperm donor* is my father too," I said, feeling the blush rise up my neck.

"Did he raise you?"

"No, but—" I began.

"Then why, Shay? He didn't care about your mother; why do you think he would care about you?"

Oh, wow. A rush of tears pushed into my eyes, but I shoved them back. I didn't have an answer for her. And what if she was right? When I'd met Mason, he hadn't known who I was. If I'd told him I was his daughter, would that have made any difference? What if I really wasn't worth caring about?

"Everything changed when your father met Jessica."

I reached for my sandwich. "What was she like, Grams?" It was a question I'd asked my aunt, too, searching for nuggets about the mom I never knew. Every single person on earth had a mother. Some were luckier than others and got to grow up with them. I thought about the moms of my friends. Tessa's mom was resilient, even if she did struggle through the devastation of her husband's infidelity. Izzy's mom valued family above all else. And like her daughter, she always gave me big hugs whenever I came over. Amelia's mom kept everyone in line and together; she was a rock the family could lean on.

Mine was a ghost. Sometimes a faint memory just out of reach. Mostly she was a creation of my mind, coming out to play in my imagination. I wished I had photos of her, because then I could picture her and how she might smile or encourage me. But beyond what little anyone had told me, I had no idea who my mother was. At least I could look Mason King up on YouTube.

I was surprised that Grams didn't immediately respond to my question. She always seemed to have an answer to everything. Instead, she took two bites of her breakfast.

"Are you sure you want me to tell you?" she finally replied.

"Of course!" I answered without thinking. But when Grams looked at me and raised an eyebrow, I wondered if I should have. I suddenly felt like I was on one of those TV lawyer shows, sitting on the witness stand. Grams was the defense attorney getting ready to cross-examine me. I almost smiled at the comparison. Grams could play a good lawyer.

"She was beautiful; I'll concede that," Grams said.

Maybe, then, there was hope for me yet. I'd never felt beautiful a day in my life, even when my dad called me pretty—because dads have to say that, right? Even if their daughters are ugly. I wasn't blind. I read magazines. I read books. I watched TV. Social media was full of pretty, and it clearly wasn't the word to describe me.

"How old was she when she married Dad?"

"Twenty-six." Grams was nearly finished with her omelet, somehow managing to make something I would've scarfed down in two minutes last our entire visit so far.

I was only a year or two old at that point, which would've put my mom in her early forties now if she had been alive. Same age as Tessa's mom probably. I wondered if they would've been friends. But . . . would I have even met my friends if my parents were still alive? I got sent to Riverbend because I didn't have either parent.

"Some people can't properly handle having kids," Grams said. "And I suppose your mom was most likely dealing with post-partum depression."

"What? Really?"

Grams nodded.

"Like how bad?"

"Bad enough."

This was news to me. Dad had never said anything about it, but why would he? He was more the adventure-seeking type who would rather jump off a cliff than talk about his feelings. Maybe that's why I struggled so much talking about mine. No one ever showed me how. So I kept my feelings to myself most of the time. Tessa, Izzy, and Amelia had helped me so much with that. They usually prodded me just enough to nudge me out of my shell without it feeling like torture.

I turned my focus to the street outside and the people walking past the coffee shop window. A man in a blue business suit with a small earbud nestled in his ear. A woman wearing huge sunglasses and carrying a massive water bottle. An elderly couple across the street walking a black Labrador retriever. Were they enjoying the moment, or were they worrying about something else—like me right now, sitting across from my grandmother, who was telling me crazy things about my mother as if Grams had my best interests at heart?

"Was she okay?" I asked. "Did she get help?"

Grams took a sip of her coffee and shrugged. "It's probably not my place to say anything."

"She was my mother. I deserve to know."

She studied my face. Then she said, "The truth isn't always easy to hear, Shay."

I closed my eyes for a second and prepared myself. My phone vibrated again on the table.

Holding her coffee mug with both hands, Grams leaned forward a little bit. "I wish Greg had told you."

"Grams, please. Tell me. Whatever it is." My heart suspected something bad was coming and stepped up its beat.

"Like I said, Jessica struggled immensely. I do not believe your father understood how much. But I could see it on her face and in how she carried herself."

"Struggled how?"

"You can't stuff intense feelings forever," Grams said, ignoring my question. "And once those feelings exploded? Well, by then it was too late for Greg to do anything."

Chapter
7

NOW SHE WAS SCARING ME. The inner Shay screamed that I should stop this conversation right now and forget I ever asked the question. Abort mission and chalk it up to curiosity not always being a good thing. Some things were better left in the past, right?

No. Even though apparently no one thought I could handle this, I could, and I needed to. I handled a whole lot more than anyone realized some days. Tessa would probably tell me I shouldn't, that I should ask for help and support from people who cared about me and could help carry the load.

I felt determination grow inside me, and I rested my arms on the table and looked my grandmother straight in the face.

"Grams, what happened to my mom?"

My grandmother wouldn't look at me. The piercing way she normally nailed me with her eyes had disappeared, and in its place was an unusual hesitation that made me want to sink into the floor.

"I think she did love you," Grams said gently. "But like I said, she struggled."

She thinks *Mom loved me?* What was she talking about? "Struggled with what?" I asked. *Loving me?*

"I may be the wrong person to share this, but . . ."

Without warning, I felt tears rush into my eyes. *No. Please. Not something else bad.* I changed my mind. I wasn't sure I could handle it after all. My heart warred with itself. But curiosity won. "I want to know," I said.

She gave a small nod and seemed to regain the determination I so often saw in her. "I don't know how to phrase this any other way, Shay."

"Just say it, Grams."

"Your mom left."

I stared at her, uncomprehending. *Left to pick up groceries? To go for a run? To get her hair done? To visit Texas?*

"About a year after they were married, she left Greg. And you." Grams sighed and gave a small shrug, as if to say, *Don't shoot the messenger.*

My heart was pounding. "Where did she go?"

"That was something we were never able to determine."

"But she came back, right?"

The wrinkles on my grandmother's forehead deepened. "She did not."

I gaped at her, then found my words. "She wouldn't do that. She wasn't like that."

"Shay, you didn't even know her."

Tell me about it! I'd spent my whole life wishing I *had*. Dad rarely spoke about her. I didn't ask him many questions because I could see how much the memories hurt. So I grew up trying to collect clues wherever I could. I desperately wanted to know *anything* about my mother—the woman who gave birth to me. But *this*? Not *this*.

Wait. Maybe Grams wasn't telling me the truth. What if she'd made it all up? But of all her faults, making things up wasn't one of them. She was clueless about teenagers, callous around people, but she wasn't a liar. She told the truth even if it came out cruel. As awful as her words could be, I didn't think the inflicted pain was ever on purpose. But that's what this information was—cruel. Wrong. Unfair. I reached across the table and grabbed my phone. Grams didn't stop me. I clambered to my feet, nearly knocking my chair over, and ran toward the bathroom.

If I stayed any longer, I'd make a scene. I'd either start crying and not be able to stop or say something stupid for Kelsey and Jade to post somewhere. Not that it mattered. Whatever they'd overheard could still be fuel for last year's fire.

I closed myself in a bathroom stall and stood there, shaking. I wanted to cry. There might be something comforting in that release.

But I couldn't.

Instead, I slammed the bottom of my fist against the stall. The pain of the impact let me know this wasn't a bad dream.

I sat silent in Grams's car as she drove me back to Booked Up. I was a quiet person in general, but this silence was different. I felt like I *couldn't* talk. The crazy part was, Grams wouldn't *stop* talking. About dumb, silly stuff. Her expansive flower garden, the fancy dinner she was cooking for guests, all the things she was planning for their summer vacation at the cottage, how she didn't like to wear the color pink but her girlfriends said it brought out her skin tone. She went on and on. It seemed like sharing this secret had opened a dam of thoughts in her head, and they came rushing out without a filter.

She stopped the SUV in the small parking lot behind the bookstore, and I felt like a robot as I climbed out.

"You'll consider what we discussed?" Grams said.

I stared at her.

"About coming to the cottage?" she continued.

I grunted something in response, shut the door, and walked toward the wooden stairs leading to the second-floor apartment. Aunt Laura was probably busy in the bookstore, which was fine with me. I needed to process the bomb my grandmother had dropped on me.

Stanley met me at the door, wagging his tail and wiggling his body. I dropped to my knees and wrapped my arms around him. For a second, he stopped his movement and stood still, a little gift to me. Then he was off, bounding across the apartment to find a toy I could throw for him. He still had a little bit of a limp but was perfectly healthy otherwise.

"Aunt Laura?" I called out.

No response.

I plopped onto the sofa in the living room and pulled out my phone. The girls had sent me a bunch of texts. The last one I had sent was the Uh, not good reply.

Understatement of the year.

"Oh, Stanley," I said. "What am I gonna do?"

Returning with a plush stuffed lion I'd given him for Christmas, the greyhound eyed me with the toy dangling from his mouth. On a different day, I might've burst out laughing.

Another text came in.

Amelia: Shay! Are you alive?????

I finally typed a response.

Me: Sry, Grams took my phone.

I scrolled through the older texts on the thread.

Tessa: Let us know how it goes.

Izzy: I'm praying!

Another text popped up.

Amelia: What?? Why'd she do that?

I tapped at the screen. Wanted to talk and didn't want me on the phone.

Amelia: About . . . ????

My friends were not what I would describe as nosy, but sometimes they got up in my business more than I liked. To them it seemed natural, something friends did. And maybe it was. I hadn't had many close friends, so I didn't always know how these things worked. Every day, I was figuring it out as I went. Although I felt a zing of irritation, I had to remind myself that I had invited them into this one.

Me: Family stuff.

Tessa: Ugh.

Yeah, she'd understand. Her dad had done what he did as a Christian, claiming it was God's best. Tessa's baby brother, Logan, was the only positive result, and Tessa had originally struggled to accept him. Would Tessa understand what my grandmother had shared? How could anyone when *I* barely did?

Tessa: Are you okay?

The truth would be *no*.

Me: Not sure.

Izzy: ☹

Amelia: What happened?

Me: G told me some stuff about my mom.

Amelia: Like . . . ???

I sunk back into the sofa and stared at the screen. I could try to reframe this all I wanted, but there was no easy way to repeat what my grandmother had told me. I simply couldn't push the revelation past my comprehension. Silly me. I thought Grams was going to tell me Mom had to be on meds for a while or something like that. Something that must have been hard at the time, but ultimately no big deal. But *this*? There was no way to process this sketchy information.

Me: 🌀 Just stuff.

Tessa: Do you want to talk about it?

Good question. If I couldn't push the words out even for me to examine them, how could I articulate it for others—even my closest friends?

Amelia: We're your friends. We want to know!

Did I want them to know? I did. But I didn't. I felt embarrassed. Once again, the girl with the weird, offbeat family situation.

I got up and went into my small bedroom and dug out the photo that Aunt Laura gave me last year. It was of my mom and dad holding me. There was my mother's smiling face right next to my pudgy kid one. She didn't *look* unhappy. I would never have guessed that probably a few short months after this was taken, she would abandon her baby—me. Her family.

I had the sudden impulse to shred the photo into a million pieces and toss it out the window for the birds to find. Let those fragments of a happy, joyful family scatter in the wind, for all I cared. My phone vibrated again, and I had the urge to toss it, too.

Tessa: I'll be at the bookstore later.

Izzy: Aw, wish I could come!

Amelia: Are you mad?

I didn't want to text anymore, but Amelia apparently took my silence in a way I didn't intend.

Me: Not mad.

Amelia: You never respond!

I had literally *just* responded to them. I wanted to type: *If I don't spill my guts about everything like you do, that doesn't mean I'm mad.*

Izzy: It's okay. You don't have to talk.

Me: Sry, bad time.

I tossed my phone onto my bed and flopped down beside it. Staring up at the ceiling with the cracks in the paint, my eyes burned with tears. First the farm, now this.

The tears silently dripped down my cheeks as I ignored the texts lighting up my phone screen.

Chapter
8

I MUST HAVE DRIFTED OFF because I woke with a jolt when my aunt's cat, Matilda, jumped onto my chest. I was still lying on my back on my bed, cell phone near my hand. I grabbed it and groaned at the number of texts I'd missed.

"My friends are ridiculous," I mumbled to Matilda and rolled off the bed, leaving her to curl up in a ball on my pillow. She often roamed the bookstore and greeted customers. Her favorite napping spot was the display window that looked out on the street. Her calm presence lured people to linger at the window. Sometimes they would come in and browse afterward, having felt a sudden urge to be as cozy and restful as a cat.

I stood in my bedroom for a second and waited for my grandmother's conversation to settle in my heart again. As my brain woke up, the weight pressed down harder.

Mom abandoned us.

She left.

Never came back.

I supposed the next time my dad heard from her, it was to find out she'd been in a car accident and was rushed to the hospital. She died two days later.

What had been going through her head when she left? Who *did* that to her husband and child? Had she intended to come back and was only trying to get her life together first? I figured I should talk to my aunt about all this. She might have clearer answers than my grandmother could give me, but just like I didn't really want to talk to my friends, I didn't have the courage to ask Aunt Laura either. I wasn't sure I wanted to know something that would shatter the precious little of the world I had left.

I made my way down the steps into the bookstore. The apartment had two entrances, one from the outside and this one, which came up directly from the store.

Afternoons in the summer could be hit or miss with customers. Weather played a big part. A nice, beautiful, sunny day had a lot of people thinking of anything but closing themselves in a room full of books. But if it was raining or the temperature turned blistering, a cozy or air-conditioned bookstore was quite the draw.

Booked Up wasn't exactly a Barnes & Noble with pristine shelves and all the newest bestsellers. My aunt kept the store stocked with the most important books for sure, but she also mixed in used titles with the new. They couldn't be ratty copies, and she paid people fairly for their lightly used books.

I walked down the self-help aisle, and a copy of the old book *How to Win Friends and Influence People* practically laughed at me. The only reason I had any friends at all was that I'd been forced to take that drama class last year. And if the extroverted Amelia and Izzy hadn't managed to wrangle Tessa and me into their fold, there was a chance I'd still be the weird loner who got nervous saying hi to someone she didn't know.

"Pardon me, miss?"

I turned around. An older woman with a cane approached me.

"Do you work here?"

"Uh . . . yes," I said.

"Can you point me to the bathroom?"

"It's at the other end of the store, past the register." I gestured in the direction.

"Thank you, dear."

I wasn't sure where my aunt was, but I hadn't come down to see her anyway. I came because I needed a distraction. Something to get my mind off everything that spun around in it. I had always enjoyed reading. After all, my dad had designed book covers for a living. So we always had books lying around, and I was reading chapter books by myself by the time I was four. Before I met Tessa, Amelia, and Izzy, books had been my closest friends. In them, I could be anything I wanted, go anywhere, see anything. In my imagination, I was strong and beautiful and confident. I could run alongside Alec and the black stallion and not grow tired. I could wield a bow next to Susan, queen of Narnia, and not be shy. I could shine a flashlight up a dark staircase with Nancy Drew and figure out who the bad guy was with ease. I could stand shoulder to shoulder with Harry, Hermione, and Ron and not be afraid.

As I grew older, I read more complicated stories, a lot of thrillers and mysteries because those were my dad's specialty as a designer. I didn't always understand the author's point, but I did enjoy the process of discovery. My dad wouldn't let me read some of the books because apparently I wasn't old enough.

"They'll be too upsetting," he'd say.

I believed him and never thought about disobeying and sneaking those books off his bookshelves to read in secret. I tried to be a good girl. I really did. But when Dad died, I felt some of that goodness die with him. Pleasing him had motivated me. Who *didn't* like to make their father proud? But now? Who would care whether I walked the straight and narrow? Yeah, my aunt wanted me to stay out of trouble, and I wasn't looking to mess up. But no matter how hard I tried, I was never going to be the girl I was before he died. A parent dying changed you in ways that were impossible to understand until you experienced them.

I wandered into the fiction room, my favorite area. Even the smell seemed different. Maybe the used pocket paperbacks brought some sort of yellowed-glue scent.

Aunt Laura divided the fiction by genre and then alphabetized by author within each section—mystery, sci-fi, fantasy, and so on. The biggest section was romance. I didn't really know anything about it since I'd never been into that genre.

When I worked a shift, sometimes my job was to rearrange any titles that were out of place. Today, as I walked slowly through the romance section looking for out-of-place titles, I spotted a *P* author in the *M* section. I slid out the book.

What I saw on the cover made my face instantly flush. A barely dressed man and woman were . . . well . . . it was pretty clear what they were doing. I knew I should probably put the book away and run, but I was riveted.

Being raised by a single dad had a lot of fun moments, but it also had its limits. Dad tried, and he gave me the basic rundown on girl stuff like periods and hormones. But I remember how uncomfortable it made him to talk about any of it. His cheeks got red, and he'd clear his throat whenever I asked questions. Eventually, I decided not to embarrass him and stopped asking.

I glanced around to see if anyone was watching, but I was alone. Something inside screamed for me to put the book back, but I didn't. Nothing in my life seemed fair right now, and it certainly didn't seem fair that I didn't have a mom to answer "girl" questions. I bet even Izzy knew more about—I glanced at the book cover—*this* kind of stuff than I did.

I think it was my frustration that made me open the book and read the first chapter. I was sick and tired of being the good girl, the quiet girl, the girl who sat in a corner and took whatever came. Why didn't anyone think about how things would affect me? Janie didn't bother to warn me about the farm. Didn't my grandmother know how her news about my mother would make me feel? What I really wanted to do was contact my biological father, but was that another stupid move? I had way too many complex emotions and no idea what to do with any of them.

I finished the chapter while standing among the shelves—almost in an act of defiance against everything that had happened in the past two days. When I finished, I had even more complex feelings than I bargained for. I was shocked at the graphic descriptions of things I'd only wondered about, but I also felt an intense curiosity to read more.

I closed the book, my heart pounding.

I shouldn't have read it.

I should have put the book away.

I knew better.

My dad would be so disappointed in me.

God would be too.

"Hey."

I jumped at the voice beside me.

"Oh, gosh, Shay. Sorry."

It was Tessa. She looked like she'd come straight from the pool, wearing a loose T-shirt and gym shorts and smelling faintly of chlorine.

I started to smile at my friend, then realized I was still holding the racy book. I quickly shoved it onto the shelf and hoped my face wasn't as flushed as it felt.

"Alphabetizing," I said. "People mess these up all the time."

Tessa paused. "That's the *M* section."

It took me a second to realize what she was saying. "Oh, right." I let out a small, totally fake laugh. The author's last name started with *P*.

"Good catch," I said.

I quickly grabbed the book and shelved it where it belonged. Had she seen me reading it?

"Your aunt carries that type of book?" Tessa's eyebrows rose.

I tried to laugh again. Wasn't that obvious? If she didn't, they wouldn't be on the shelves. "Guess so," I said, quickly moving into the mystery aisle, hoping Tessa would follow.

She did, but apparently she wasn't finished with the subject.

"It's just that . . ."

"What?"

Tessa fingered her car keys, a blush creeping up her neck. "I think those have a lot of . . . gross stuff in them."

My face grew hotter too. I focused on the shelf next to me where copies of Sue Grafton's alphabet series sat. *A Is for Alibi, B Is for Burglar* . . .

Tessa sighed. "I don't understand why people read them."

C Is for Corpse . . . D Is for Deadbeat . . .

"Me either," I said.

"So, are you okay?"

"Yeah, I'm fine."

Both of my responses grated on my conscience because, of all my friends, Tessa was the one who'd taken the time to get to know me best. Izzy and I had spent time together too, but that time was lighter, less deep. More about connecting over pop culture and eating junk food. But Tessa had come over to the apartment to spend the night and watch a meteor shower last November. We'd talked about stuff then that was vulnerable and real. What if I told her what was actually going on?

"What happened with your grandmother?" she prodded.

I told her a little about the meeting and how I'd felt, but I stopped short of the big reveal about my mom. That still seemed too raw.

Tessa touched my shoulder. "I'm sorry."

"It's not *your* fault."

"Yeah, but I know what family stuff feels like."

I laughed, and this time it was genuine. "You totally do."

"I wish I could stay longer," she said. "But Mom wants us to do dinner and a movie."

My heart fell a little. It was so nice to talk with someone who cared about me, even if only for a minute. Our spontaneous morning snack yesterday had made me miss my friends even more.

"Maybe I could—" I started to say "come too" but then realized I would probably be intruding on their mother/daughter thing. I swallowed the tightening in my throat and forced a smile. "Maybe I could see you later."

"Yeah, definitely," Tessa said, giving me a quick hug.

And then she was gone, and I was left standing alone among the books that told so many stories yet could do nothing to help mine.

Chapter
9

"How was your day?"

Aunt Laura walked into the apartment and immediately went to the refrigerator. She grabbed a Diet Coke, popped the can, and took a long sip. She wore a nineties rock band T-shirt over black jeans but somehow still looked professional.

"Fine," I said.

"Uh-oh."

My aunt came to where I was sitting on the sofa. Stanley had fallen asleep beside me, his head on my leg. I stroked the top of his head, and little multicolored dog hairs fell to the sofa cushion beside us. I hadn't been able to move for the past twenty minutes. This greyhound had come into my life at the right time, and I was so thankful he was staying permanently.

"Not very convincing, kiddo."

"It was fine."

Aunt Laura plopped down beside me, and Stanley thumped

his tail twice. She rested her head back on the cushion, closing her eyes for a second. Owning and running the bookstore had been a dream come true for her, something she'd fantasized about as a kid ever since watching *Beauty and the Beast* and longing for Belle's library. But it wasn't all rainbows and roses. Some months she barely scratched out enough to pay her lease, and every year she was just glad the store survived in a world where physical books weren't treasured like they used to be.

Aunt Laura eyed me. "So, I'm assuming things didn't go well with your grandmother."

I shrugged, still stroking Stanley's head. He sighed and rolled onto his back, lifting one front leg into the air. For such big dogs, greyhounds could contort into the strangest positions.

"Shay, I know you're not fine."

I focused on my lap and tried not to cry.

"Do you want to talk about it?" my aunt asked.

"Not really," I said.

She nodded. "Okay, fair enough."

Even though I said I didn't want to talk, I wished I could bare everything to my aunt. I was pretty sure she could handle it, but what if she didn't know the details about Mom leaving? She had to have known Mom left. And I certainly didn't want to bring up a subject that could be painful to her as well. Yet I also didn't know how long I could keep this stuff to myself.

"Full disclosure." Aunt Laura set her Diet Coke on a coaster. "Your grandmother called me."

I sighed. "When?"

"Earlier today."

So *after* our little "chat." Terrific. It wouldn't be the first time Aunt Laura had to listen to my grandmother complain about me. But I was glad she had asked for my side of things before making any judgments.

"We need to remember how she's helped us," Aunt Laura said.

"What did she say?" I asked.

"I just wanted to remind you of that first." My aunt pointed at Stanley, still lying on his back beside me. "His life certainly would be different without her help . . . if he was alive at all."

She was right, but I was getting tired of using that as an excuse for my grandmother's less-than-nice behavior. Sometimes I felt like she'd only done that to buy my loyalty, but then I remembered she had paid for the surgery anonymously.

"You going to give me more details about how it went?" Aunt Laura asked.

I shrugged again.

"That good, huh?"

"She's never easy to talk to."

"I know, but I'm still thankful you try."

"I honestly don't feel like trying anymore."

"I get that, kiddo. But she's your family. That's important."

"I'm not family—according to her sometimes."

My aunt paused, perhaps remembering that dinner conversation where my grandmother had all but said I wasn't family because I was adopted.

"Shay, she doesn't mean those things."

"Then she shouldn't say them."

I started to stand, but my aunt caught hold of my arm. "Wait."

I resisted the urge to pull away. "If I were her real granddaughter, she would treat me differently. Maybe she'd actually love me."

"She does love you."

"Then why am I even *here*? In this apartment. With you." My voice was rising. I tried to dial it back down. "Sorry, it's . . ." I began, but my voice trailed off.

"Go ahead. You're allowed to say what you want—respectfully," my aunt said.

I decided to give her a little of what I was feeling. "She said stuff about Mom."

"Like . . . ?"

This time I did stand, letting Stanley's head slip off my leg and onto the sofa cushion. I needed to do something with the frenetic emotions inside me. Whenever I was with Grams, I felt like I was constantly playing Whac-A-Mole with my feelings, but here Aunt Laura was asking me to talk, and I couldn't do that either. Not like she wanted me to, anyway.

"She wants me to go up to their cottage with them."

"Okay."

"But I don't want to."

"Kid, if I had my way you wouldn't have to do anything you didn't want to do." Aunt Laura looked up at me, and I knew she meant it. It was a small relief.

"Is that what she called about?" I asked.

My aunt sighed.

"I don't want to go," I said.

Aunt Laura stood up too. "I'll give you that your grandmother isn't the easiest person in the world to deal with."

"For reals."

"But . . ." My aunt held up a finger to make me pause. "You still need to respect her."

"Is it disrespectful if I don't want to go to the cottage? Does respecting her mean I have to do everything she wants?"

Aunt Laura paused, considering. "My immediate response is 'Of course not.' But I'm trying to think through what I want to say." She paused again, and I waited—not very patiently. My anger was starting a slow boil. "It is respectful to consider her feelings about the invitation."

"How can I? She doesn't care about me!"

"You know that's not true."

I could feel tears threatening to pour from my eyes and anger threatening to pour from my mouth. Tears are where I always seem to go when I get upset. I hate crying in front of people. I'd rather lash out to chase away my tears. Of course, my aunt had seen me cry before, and she wouldn't care if I did, but *I* cared. Crying always felt like weakness. So what if crying was supposed to be therapeutic? I knew if I let go, I'd say or do something I regretted, and I didn't want to make things worse for myself.

"Your grandmother is still dealing with her grief."

"And I'm *not*?" The pressure of loss swelled in my chest.

Stanley lifted his head off the sofa and looked at me. It was as if he could sense my rising emotions. My phone was still sitting beside the dog, and right then it vibrated. Stanley cocked his head, glancing at it. I couldn't even bring myself to crack a smile at his silliness.

"That's not what I'm saying at all, sweetheart," Aunt Laura said.

Sweetheart. I think that was the first time my aunt had used that endearing term.

"It's always about her," I said. "I'm supposed to be nice, cater to everything she wants, and all she does in return is lay on the guilt."

My aunt rubbed her eyes, and a little bit of makeup smeared onto her cheek. I probably didn't tell her I appreciated her as much as I should.

"I need you to still try," she said.

"I am."

"Really?"

I almost broke down and shared everything Grams had said. I needed to know the truth about my family, and my aunt might have the pieces I was desperate to find. But something stopped me. I wasn't sure what it was at first, but then its familiar hand wrapped around my heart. *Fear.*

It seemed everyone grew tired of me at some point. My old friends, my mom, my grandmother. I was afraid my aunt would get tired of me too. What was to keep her from deciding she'd had enough moody, teen-girl vibes and wanted her old life back? The one where she didn't have to share her space with a messy niece who had to be reminded to close the cabinet doors and do her laundry. What if she no longer wanted to have to pay double for food bills and shuttle a kid around to school functions and horse barns?

"I can't force you to go to the cottage," Aunt Laura said. "And I guess you've made your decision. But I want you to seriously consider these sorts of requests, okay? Maybe your grandmother wants to spend time together because she really is trying to have a better relationship with you."

Nope. It wasn't just that I didn't want to spend time away from the horses or these girls who were my new friends. It just wasn't worth the risk—the risk of finding out Grams truly didn't like me and didn't want me around. "Fine," I responded sharply, deciding to stay quiet on everything else like I usually did. And then I stormed off to my room.

Chapter
10

THERE WEREN'T TOO MANY DAYS I wished I could drive, but today was one of them. While some teenagers count down the days until they get their driving permits, I was waiting to see how long I could go without my aunt forcing me to get mine. Both my parents had died in car accidents, and I was not eager to sit in the driver's seat. But if I had a license today, I would get in my car and drive to Green Tree Farm and bury my face in the neck of a patient horse. Probably Ava. Or maybe I'd get on the highway and drive to Ohio. Or California. Or maybe even Texas. Anywhere other than Riverbend.

Instead, taking Stanley on an evening walk would have to do.

Riverbend wasn't a huge metropolis like Columbus or San Francisco or Dallas, but it was more "city" than I was used to. I'd always be a country girl at heart, but I'd learned to appreciate walking to shops and restaurants—even school. Stanley had gotten used to it as well and enjoyed our visits to Founder's Park.

Greyhounds usually have a huge prey drive. They were bred to hunt small game like rabbits, so it was important to always keep Stanley on a leash or in a fenced-in yard. But while some dogs practically walk their owners by yanking them down the street, he calmly trotted beside me with slack in his leash. Maybe my aunt was right. I needed to be thankful Grams had helped Stanley when he needed it most.

But I could still be annoyed that my grandmother pressured me all the time.

I passed Grounds and Rounds and thought I saw Zoe, the youth leader from Izzy and Tessa's church, at a table with a bunch of teen girls. She regularly met with some of us outside youth group to offer a listening ear and biblical guidance. She'd been helping several of the girls who were caught up in the Dropbox scandal last year, including Izzy.

Izzy had been so out of sorts about it. I couldn't imagine how I would've felt if someone had taken a photo of me and photo-shopped it to look like I was naked. The guys who'd paid to view the photos of Izzy and a bunch of other girls at school had been brought in by the police, and they'd gotten in serious trouble.

Izzy had been mortified, obviously, because she would never, ever dream of sending anyone inappropriate pictures. I suppose the other girls felt awful too. Some of them had sent boys pictures of themselves, and their photos were *not* photoshopped. Sure, they were supposed to have been private messages to one person, but still.

It was all pretty gross. But then, for some reason, I remembered that novel in the bookstore and some of the things described in the first chapter. It's not like it had photos or anything. It was fiction. That was different, wasn't it?

Stanley stopped to sniff a tree trunk.

The way Tessa had talked about the book made me pause. If something bothered Tessa, I at least wanted to listen, but I wasn't sure if she understood. I hadn't done anything wrong, really. It was just a book. A made-up story.

A guy coming toward me on the sidewalk had his shirt slung over his shoulder in the heat, and I couldn't help but notice his muscular torso and six-pack abs. He could be a model for the covers of those novels. He smiled at me as he passed, and I looked away.

Before I knew it, I'd walked through town into the small neighborhood where Tessa now lived. She was still getting used to the much smaller house, but her mom seemed to appreciate the cozier space. Not to mention it was probably a lot cheaper than their old place.

Stanley lifted his leg on a bush, and I took a moment to watch the house. Not in a creeper kind of way, but just thinking about my friend and her life. The sun was starting to set, and lights were on in the windows. I hadn't expected to see Tessa, but I caught sight of her in the kitchen, and there was her mom, too, laughing at something.

It had been a long time since Mrs. Hart seemed to have any joy in her life, so I was glad to see her and Tessa sharing the moment. Would my mom and I have moments like that if she were still alive? What would that be like? What if she'd married Mason King instead of my dad? Maybe then my dream of training horses wouldn't be simply a dream. I might be the one in the arena with my father. If he'd had a daughter to care for, maybe he would be different too. What if the issues in his life that caused him to be aggressive with Ava wouldn't have materialized if he and Mom had stayed together?

A deep longing for what could have been hit me, and it surprised me how powerful the feeling was. Dang it. Why was I so emotional lately? It's not as if I'd had a bad childhood. Dad had been a *good* father and given me everything I needed. But the yearning for belonging in an ordinary family—beyond one parent, or aunt—hit me hard. Tessa had her mom, but she also still had her dad, and now she had a brother—even if she didn't get along with her stepmother.

Stanley walked over to another bush. "Come on, boy. We gotta get you home."

But Stanley wasn't ready, and neither was I. I could still see Tessa and her mom. It looked like they were cooking dinner. Tessa was at the sink, and her mom came up behind her and said something that made Tessa smile. Then her mom hugged her—not a light, perfunctory little squeeze. Mrs. Hart held on to her daughter for a few seconds, and when she let go, I felt my emotions well up again.

I considered knocking on their door but decided I needed to let them have their time. I should go. If I didn't leave now, I'd end up a sobbing mess in front of my friend's house.

"Hey there."

I nearly jumped out of my skin at the voice behind me. I swung around. A tall teen boy with curly dark hair stood there, a dainty black poodle on a leash beside him. Stanley eyed the dog. I kept my eyes on the guy. For a second, I didn't put two and two together, but then I quickly remembered I'd met him before.

"Abraham, was it?"

"That's me." Abraham gave a little mock bow and gestured toward the dog. "And my charge, Maxine."

I *did* remember his dog. I wanted to kneel and say hello to her, but I wasn't sure how Stanley would react, so I remained standing.

"Can they say hi?" Abraham pointed to my greyhound.

"Um . . . I guess?" That came out more like a question.

"Maxine won't bite."

"It's not her I'm worried about. I'm not sure about Stanley." I nodded at my dog.

Abraham laughed. It was a nice, real laugh, and I realized it was exactly what I needed. My thoughts had spiraled way too much while looking at Tessa and her mom.

We let the dogs sniff noses first, and Stanley's tail started wagging. So did Maxine's.

"See?" Abraham said. "They like each other."

"Greyhounds don't always get along with small dogs," I said.

He nodded. "But they're sighthounds. Hear that, Maxine? Don't run and you'll be fine."

I was surprised he knew enough about dogs to even know what a sighthound was. *Props to you, Abraham.*

"You visiting Tessa?" he asked.

The dogs had moved to sniffing each other all over, their ears happy and perked, tails still wildly flapping.

"No, just out walking."

He smiled. "Good way to clear your head. Isn't that right, Maxine?" The poodle looked up at the mention of her name but then quickly returned her focus to Stanley. In size comparison, the two dogs looked like a giraffe and a tiger standing next to each other.

"Or get stuck in it," I said in a quiet voice.

"Yeah, that too."

I kept my eyes on the dogs, surprised Abraham so readily agreed and seemed to understand. Tessa had warned me about him being a flirt, and I wondered if I would even recognize flirtation if I saw it. Although I was raised by a single dad, I didn't know much about boys. Definitely not teenage ones.

Abraham nodded toward Tessa's house. "I'm glad she seems happy after all the stuff she's dealt with."

"Me too. She deserves it." I meant that with all my heart. Even if I felt twinges of jealousy, I'd never want any of my friends to experience bad things just so we could commiserate with each other.

"What about you?" Abraham asked. Maxine pulled against her leash, but Abraham held it steady.

"What do you mean?"

"You live with your aunt, right?"

"Mmhmm."

"Mom? Dad?"

I couldn't remember if Abraham went to our school or not. If he did, he probably would've heard about me already—thanks to Jade and Kelsey.

"Neither," I said. "They're both dead."

He grunted a little in apparent understanding. I glanced at his face, and there was no hint of teasing or blowing me off. He seemed incredibly genuine, and I didn't know what to do with that. I'd never had much interest in dating, mostly because I had no clue how any of that even worked, but I wouldn't mind being friends with a guy.

"My parents are divorced," he said. "Both remarried. Some days I wonder if it would've been easier if I was in your shoes instead."

I gave him an incredulous look. "Seriously?"

"Sorry, I don't mean to sound like I have it harder."

"No, I . . . I think I get it," I said.

"But live life to the full, you know? No matter what's happened. Make your own life. That's what I'm trying to do."

I watched the dogs play and wondered what I could do to "make my own life." Instead of allowing life to control me, what if I took the bull by the horns and made strong decisions that would change my destiny?

"Well, I guess I better get going," Abraham said. "Say hi to Tessa for me."

We had to practically pry our dogs apart, which made us both laugh. As he walked away, I almost thanked Abraham for taking a minute to really *see* me, but I didn't. That would sound weird. I was awkward enough already.

I pulled out my phone and sent a text as I walked, a smile still on my face.

Me: Hope u r having a great time w/ your mom!

Within a minute, Tessa texted back.

Tessa: I am! How are you?

Me: OK!

Technically, I had to admit, it was true. With all I'd lost, I'm sure some people would wonder how I could be happy. Still, I had a roof over my head, a cute dog and cat to love, and an aunt who was trying her best. I should be grateful. Even if my mom had been different from how I'd imagined her, I hadn't had a horrible childhood. I'd been doing okay until Dad died and my world blew apart. And honestly, compared to losing my dad and being forced to move away from my home, how big of a deal should it be for the farm to sell, and for me to lose my job?

I passed Grounds and Rounds right as Zoe was walking out. She held some sort of green iced drink. There was no time for me to avoid her before she saw me.

"Hi!" she said, all sunshine and sparkles. How did she *do* that? I had never seen her be anything but upbeat. I used to think she was acting fake, but Tessa said it was real.

"How ya doing, girl?" Zoe flipped her braids over her shoulder and shifted her purse. "Still working with horses?"

"Yeah." *For now.*

"That's cool, Shay. I know you love that."

I distracted myself by wondering which girls she'd met with today and what they'd discussed. I enjoyed deep conversations, but not necessarily with Zoe. She had a way of zeroing in on hard stuff. That was her job in a lot of ways, but it still made me uncomfortable.

"Summer's kind of been . . ." I hesitated to say what I wanted. It's not as if Zoe and I were friends or anything. But maybe . . . youth leaders had to keep confidences, right?

Zoe smiled. "Want to sit down?"

I started to protest because of Stanley. The last time I tried to bring him into the coffee shop, I got asked to leave. But Zoe remembered and gestured toward one of the tables outside.

"I guess I can sit for a minute," I said.

We walked over to a black, cast-iron table with an umbrella and sat down. Stanley lay on the cement beside me, panting. He was probably glad for the break in our walk anyway.

"So, tell me about your summer." Zoe pulled some of the green drink up with her straw, looking truly interested.

Before I could stop myself, I blurted out that the farm was being sold and I had no idea what I was going to do for the rest of the summer since I didn't want to go to my grandparents' cottage. "I don't understand why God would let that happen to me. I just got back on my feet, you know?"

Zoe half whistled, half breathed out a long breath. "That's the question of the ages, girl."

"It's not fair," I said.

"Totally isn't."

Okay . . . I hadn't expected her to agree with me.

"Hey, I'm not going to go all youth pastor on you," Zoe said with a smile. "But I will tell you that God isn't afraid of your questions."

Well, that was good to know, because I had a lot of them.

I was suddenly telling Zoe more. "I just found out my mom left me and my dad when I was a baby."

Her eyes widened. "Wow, Shay, that's tough."

"It makes me wonder if she ever loved me." A tear leaked out of my eye and dripped down my cheek. I swiped it away, hoping Zoe hadn't seen but knowing she had.

"Oh, girl." Zoe reached across the table and grabbed my hand. "Don't go there. You're going to torture yourself."

"What kind of mom does that?"

Zoe didn't hesitate. "One who is hurting," she said. "And we can be almost certain that it had nothing to do with you."

I wanted to believe her. But she knew nothing of my mom's heart. None of us did. She could be right, but she also might not be. My mom could've regretted ever having me, and that possibility was more than I could bear.

"Do you have my number?" Zoe asked.

I shrugged. I didn't think I did.

"Here, give me your phone."

I was too tired to protest, so I handed it over. Zoe punched her name and number into my contacts.

"Can I have yours too?" she asked.

I gave it to her.

"You can contact me anytime," she told me.

She waited for me to continue talking, but I was done. There was nothing more to say. I got up, and with a wave and a thank-you, took Stanley home. I walked through the bookstore on the way up to the apartment, and before my conscience could scold me, I passed through the romance section and found the book I'd started earlier.

I hid it under my bed.

Chapter
11

LATER THAT NIGHT, I crawled under my sheets and stared up at the ceiling. True darkness hadn't come yet, as the summer evenings extended far beyond their winter counterparts. I was exhausted but in that awful place of desperately longing for rest yet unable to fall asleep. Stanley lay on his bed beside mine. In the winter, he'd curl up with me, but when it was hot, he sprawled alone on the floor.

The air-conditioning unit in my window chugged away trying to cool us down, but it was old, and the air was incredibly hot. Even with it running all night, I still woke up sweating. Aunt Laura was awake in the living room, probably on the couch watching a TV show. I thought about Zoe and how willing she'd been to talk to me. I knew my aunt would be the same, but did I want to risk it?

I slipped out of bed and crept out. Yep, my aunt was lying on the sofa. Matilda lay stretched out on the back of the cushions near her. I went over to them and plopped down on the end of the sofa by Aunt Laura's feet.

She flipped her iPad onto her chest. "Hey, you."

I curled up and let my head fall onto the armrest.

"Can't sleep?"

"It's cooler out here."

"Your A/C still not working right?"

"No."

"I'll replace it as soon as I can."

"It's okay."

I closed my eyes. Once in a blue moon when I was little, Dad and I would fall asleep on the couch watching old Disney movies. I remember waking up the mornings after, believing my dad was the best dad in the world. A tiny smile snuck in. Well, he did die before we got to experience a lot of teenage drama. For the most part, I'd been a pretty obedient kid and didn't get into trouble. Why did it seem like now everything was changing?

"Grams said a lot of things I didn't tell you," I finally admitted.

Aunt Laura set her iPad on the end table and focused on me.

"About Mom," I said. "Some not-nice things."

My aunt shook her head. "That woman." She sat up. "What did she say?"

"Grams didn't want Dad to marry Mom, did she?"

"Your grandmother is a very opinionated person. And her opinions can be stark. Rather black-and-white." She stuffed a throw pillow behind her back. "And no, she didn't want them to marry."

"Why not? Was something wrong with Mom?"

"You have to understand that your dad was your grandmother's only son—her only *child*. In some ways, she treated him like one even when he was an adult."

That was a weird way to imagine my father, but I didn't want to follow that bunny trail. I wanted to stay on track, and I felt like my aunt was avoiding the question. I tried to rephrase it. "What about her didn't she like?"

Aunt Laura pinched the bridge of her nose. "It's late, Shay."

Did that mean she wasn't going to talk to me?

"I don't understand. I want to."

"You're right. She didn't like your mom."

I repositioned myself on the sofa. Matilda yawned and stretched, curling into a different cushion. "Please tell me, Aunt Laura."

"Is this something you need to know right now?"

I'd asked myself the same question the entire day. All I'd wanted was to enjoy breakfast with my grandmother and maybe chat about dumb, teenage things. Talk a little about horses maybe. But now that my grandmother had brought it up, the topic of my mom had become as compelling as the desire to contact Mason King.

Parents were the biggest part of who a kid was. I totally got now how some people who were adopted, even if they grew up in a happy family and were well loved, wanted to know where they came from. Maybe it was a preprogrammed need to understand their history so they could make sense of their present. I'd tried to convince myself I didn't need those puzzle pieces. But it hadn't worked. I couldn't deny I needed them.

The problem was, once you knew something, you couldn't unknow it, like my aunt had told me once. And it was worse to have only partial answers.

Aunt Laura rubbed her eyes and let out a groan. "Oh, Shay, I'm not trying to avoid your questions or make this hard for you, but I don't want you to get hurt any more than you already have."

"Did Mom leave?" I blurted.

I watched my aunt's face. Her jaw muscle twitched, and she looked me right in the eyes. It was almost like I could see and hear the war going on in her mind. *Answer Shay or not. Truth or a sidestep.*

Aunt Laura's face became grim. "That decision was the worst one she ever made."

"So she did leave?"

"It had absolutely nothing to do with you."

"Is that what she told you?"

"Your mother and I did not agree on everything, and we certainly argued a lot in the days before she made the decision to leave. She was saying all kinds of stupid things. Although I had no idea what all her crazy talk was leading up to." Aunt Laura sat up and scooted closer to me on the sofa. "Jessica only talked to me once after she left, and that was to ask me for money I didn't have."

"She just left?" Would asking more than once make it any less true?

"I don't know what she was thinking, Shay," Aunt Laura said. "But I do know she loved you. You were her world."

"Yeah, I can see that."

Aunt Laura touched my arm for a second. "I know that's hard to believe, but there is far more to the story than even I know."

"Grams said she had depression."

"I think that's true. That's part of what we argued about. I mean, I didn't label it as depression at the time, but I kept pushing her to get help." Aunt Laura stared at something on the floor, and for a second, I thought I saw her eyes water. "I could have been a better sister to her too. I got so annoyed, I stopped answering her phone calls."

"Didn't she love my dad?"

"These are very difficult questions to answer." My aunt pulled her legs back up onto the sofa and reached over to stroke Matilda's back. The cat gave her hand a small lick and then returned to her napping. "The answers are almost too complicated to convey all that happened."

"Why don't parents *think* before they go mess everything up?"

My voice sounded more bitter than I intended. I hoped my aunt wasn't mad at me, but when I looked over at her, she only seemed sad.

"I hear you." Aunt Laura winced as she spoke. "I don't know a lot, kid, but I know your mom did her best. Was that always good enough? No. And unfortunately, she's not here to answer you. We can only guess. But, Shay?"

I looked over at my aunt. She wore no makeup and a baggy T-shirt over gym shorts, but in that moment, she was the most important person in my world, and I wanted to hear whatever she wanted to say.

Aunt Laura smiled at me. "I'm not going anywhere, okay?"

I wiped my eyes and nodded.

"And I'm gonna mess up too," she said. "I don't know what I'm doing sometimes, but I'm trying."

"Me too," I said.

My aunt gave my leg a quick pat. "That's all we *can* do."

Chapter

12

AFTER TALKING WITH AUNT LAURA, I climbed back into bed, feeling a mixture of relief and sadness. But I couldn't fall asleep. Even after the kindness of my aunt, my brain wouldn't stop rehashing and re-sorting everything. I pulled out my phone and contemplated telling my friends about my mother. Maybe they'd understand.

Me: Can't sleep.

I stared at the screen and waited.

No responses.

My screen went black.

I woke it up again.

Saw the clock.

No wonder. It was after midnight. All three of them probably had their phones on silent or were too sound asleep to hear.

Like I should have been.

I groaned and rested my arm over my eyes.

A minute later, I startled when my phone vibrated in my hand.

Izzy: Me either. Ugh.

Me: Why for you?

Izzy: Drank coffee.

Me: What????

Izzy: Big mistake.

Me: Thought u hated it.

Izzy: Definitely do now! LOL

Me: Silly.

Izzy: My brain is whirring!

Me: Mine too.

I thought about the talk I'd had with Zoe.

Me: Do u talk to Zoe much?

Izzy: Sure.

I stared at my phone screen. We hadn't spent much time discussing what happened to her with the photo scandal. I'd avoided asking Izzy about it mostly for her privacy, but it also made me uncomfortable. I decided to give her a chance to open up.

Me: About what?

I sent the text but then wished I could take it back. It was too pushy, too personal.

Izzy: Oh, lots of things. Sebastian. Claire. The Bible.

Me: I talked to her a bit today.

Izzy: That's great!

Me: She's nice.

Izzy: I know. I love her. ♥

Well, I couldn't go *that* far, but I could see why my friends spoke well of the woman. I thought about the book under my bed, and I slipped out of the sheets and reached down to grab it. My phone screen lit up the cover, and I felt an immediate flush of guilt that I even had this book in my room. But why? It was fiction. Was it really wrong? Tessa seemed to think so. Zoe probably too. But if it was so wrong, why did my aunt have the book in her store? True, she didn't buy every single book herself. An employee could've been the one to purchase it used, but Aunt Laura was generally aware of what her store stocked.

My phone vibrated in my hand again.

Tessa: I'm up.

Izzy: You too?

Me: Hey.

Hey? I closed my eyes. I could be such a dork sometimes. I hadn't owned a cell phone when Dad was alive. My grandmother got me one after I went to live with her. But I always thought of it as more for emergencies.

Tessa: Had a great time with my mom tonight!

Izzy: Yay! What did you do?

Tessa: Dinner, dessert, movie. Love seeing her happier.

I paused. Tessa had no idea that I'd seen her through the window. She also had no idea how much it hurt right now to hear about anyone else's mom. The new revelation about my mom burst me wide open. I could try to tell myself over and over that Aunt Laura was right, that my mom had loved me, that she'd been hurting, but no words could bring together the fissures of pain in my heart.

Me: I'm glad she's better. You guys needed that.

Tessa: Yeah, we did.

Izzy: You're handling things really well, Tessa.

Tessa: LOL. Doesn't feel like it. But thanks.

Izzy: I've been praying for you and your mom. ♥

Tessa: Aw, thanks.

Izzy: Zoe told me the other day that God works everything together for good.

I recoiled and hated myself for it. How could I have that reaction to a Bible verse? How could it mean that God was working when my mom left her husband and child?

I could list so many horrible things that had happened to me and others, stupid things that made no sense. And yet people had told me that God allowed my dad to die to work a greater miracle in my life. I'd wanted to punch them.

Me: God doesn't make bad stuff happen does He?

Izzy: He allows it though?

Tessa: I guess.

Me: Tough to swallow.

Izzy: I think people do bad stuff because He gives everyone choice. Free will.

Me: Not arguing, but . . .

Izzy: People do what they want and it sometimes hurts other people. ☹

I was starting to get annoyed. Like a frowny face was going to make me feel better?

Izzy: I've been trying to let go of my anger and trust that God will judge people like Zac for their actions. It's hard.

I don't know if it was because it was late or what, but the more we texted, the more I could feel my insides cramping. I'd hoped hearing from my friends would make me feel better, but I was feeling the opposite.

Me: I'm trying to let go.

Izzy: About your bio dad?

Me: Yeah, that too.

Tessa: It's rough for sure sometimes.

Me: Just found out my mom left my dad and me when I was little. Did God cause THAT?

Tessa: So sorry.

Izzy: Oh, Shay! 😭 😭 😭

Me: Yeah.

Tessa: Who told you?

Me: Grams.

Izzy: Sending hugs, Shay. ♥♥♥

I appreciated their kindness, but I wasn't sure if they really got it. Izzy's life, for example, was a heck of a lot more stable than mine. Even her brother struggling with a disability and the pressure that had put on her family wasn't enough to divide them. They had come together stronger. That same longing for a family I'd felt outside Tessa's house hit me again.

Me: So that's why I don't like a God who lets bad things happen—especially to kids.

Izzy: I get it. You've been through so much.

Me: Kinda have.

I didn't want to play the victim or for them to worry about me, but I also was tired of pretending.

Izzy: God loves you. ♥

Me: Thanks.

Tessa: Life's hard.

Izzy: Lord Jesus, please comfort Shay and give her peace and rest and understanding. We love her so much. Help her to trust You with all this.

Tessa: Amen! I'm sorry, but it's late.

Me: Yeah, good night.

Izzy: Good night, girls. Love you. ♥♥

I glanced at the novel sitting beside me on the bed. My friends had been so sweet and caring. But if they knew what I'd read, I was pretty sure that's not how they'd respond. Well. That didn't really matter because they would never know.

Chapter

13

"Shay, get up."

I tried to open my eyes, but they felt glued shut.

"Now, kid. Or you'll be late."

I managed to wake up enough to realize my aunt was hovering over me.

"What . . . time . . . is it?"

"Six o'clock."

My alarm had been set for five. How had I missed it?

Aunt Laura pulled my covers off with a swift yank, and I groaned.

"Hey, I'm not the one who committed to feeding fifty million horses."

"Fourteen," I mumbled.

"Well, those fourteen will be pretty ticked if you show up late." Aunt Laura held a coffee cup. "Not to mention that Janie lady."

I made another complaining sound.

"I'm serious, get up." My aunt walked out of the room, calling over her shoulder, "Ride leaves in ten."

Somehow I got dressed in record time, wolfed down some cereal, and grabbed a bottle of water to take with me. I met my aunt at her Jeep, and she drove me to Green Tree Farm, still sipping her coffee. This is how we rolled on the days I worked—but usually more on time.

"Thanks," I said, meaning it as I climbed out.

My aunt smiled. "Text me a ten-minute warning when you're ready to be picked up."

I waved, and then jogged inside. I could see the horses waiting at the gates, watching intently for me. They knew the drill.

Glancing into the stalls as I passed, I was relieved they were all clean and ready for their equine occupants. I set a grain pan in each stall so they'd have food as soon as they came in. Janie asked me to bring the horses in one at a time to keep things orderly and safe—even though she herself sometimes brought in two or three at once.

"Okay, Charlie. You first," I said to the big bay as I attached the ratty, well-used lead rope to his halter. The horses were a lot calmer after grazing in the field all night, so most walked politely next to me as I led them to their stalls, where I removed their fly masks and halters.

When I was done bringing in the geldings, I went to the mares' pasture to get the four mares. When I got there, three of the girls were hanging their heads over the railing near the gate, waiting semi-patiently. But I didn't see Ava. She was more timid than the rest, so she sometimes held back until the others were out of the pasture. I scanned the acreage, but I didn't see her anywhere. I felt a zing of anxiety zip through me. As I walked the first mare to the barn, my insides felt a bit scrambled and nervous. As soon as I had the chestnut mare situated, I checked Ava's stall at the very end of the row in case, in my groggy state, I'd missed her.

Empty.

Panic exploded in my chest. Had she escaped the pasture during the night? Was she running around in the woods lost? What if she had ended up on the road and gotten hit by a truck? As fast as I could, I brought in the other two mares and ran back out to the field, calling her name. Whistling. There were a few trees down by the far end. Maybe she was lying down napping. It was unlikely, as I could clearly see there were no horses down there, but still I ran down and checked, panting by the time I got there.

No Ava.

I yanked out my phone and dialed Janie. I had to get help, and fast. I didn't know if she was home or not, but worst case, I'd pound on her door.

The phone rang three times before she picked up.

"What's up, Shay?"

"I can't find Ava! What should I do?"

"Well, that was quick," Janie said.

With one hand clutching the phone to my ear, I jogged back toward the barn. "The gate was closed, but she isn't here," I said. "Could someone have stolen her?"

Would I get blamed for this? Maybe I could saddle up one of the other horses and start looking for her, but I wasn't the best rider in the world and wasn't convinced I could ride fast enough to cover any ground.

"Shay, she's gone."

"I know!"

"Her owners must have come to pick her up last night."

I stopped in my tracks. "What?"

"They wanted to get her settled at her new home as soon as possible."

"Are you kidding?" I stood there, my feet planted on the ground like a horse fixating on something it'd seen in the distance. "They came and took her without you knowing?"

"No, I knew they were coming. I just wasn't sure of the day."

"But . . . why didn't you tell me?"

"I should have. I'm sorry. I was so tied up with everything that I forgot."

"She's really *gone* for good?"

"I'm afraid so."

"Where did she go?"

"They didn't tell me, and I didn't ask."

I spun around and stared at the empty pasture. My heart ached that I hadn't had a chance to say goodbye. Janie knew I cared about that mare, probably even more than Ava's college-age owner, who rarely came to see her.

"Are the rest of the horses in?" Janie asked.

Was there any way I could find out where she'd gone? With Ava's sweet timidity, she needed someone to handle her gently and with understanding. How would the new barn staff know that she loved to have her hay right beside her water so she could dip it in as she ate? Or that she would only eat her grain if the supplements were on the *bottom* of the feed bowl and never sprinkled on top?

"Did you hear me, Shay?"

I turned back toward the barn.

"The other horses," Janie prodded. "Are they in?"

"Yeah," I mumbled.

"Chance and Snow are moving out today too."

Those were two gelding "brothers" who were inseparable in the field. If you brought one of them in to ride, you had better bring in the other, too, or else he'd be screaming in the pasture or running the fence line, disturbing everyone.

"The sale is officially a done deal," Janie said. "So we'll have to talk about how long I'll need you."

The reality of what was going to happen hit me harder than I expected. It wasn't as if I didn't realize it when she told me she was selling. The sediment had been stirred the moment she spoke those words, but it took this long for it all to settle to the bottom of my heart. My world was crumbling, and there was nothing I could do about it.

Chapter
14

I was still reeling a few minutes later and sent my friends a quick text: Ava left.

I sat on a hay bale in the middle of the barn aisle, staring at my phone. The box fans hanging on the outside of each horse stall whirred as much as my thoughts. I was alone in the barn with thirteen horses. Not fourteen. And soon it was going to be eleven.

My phone vibrated as a text came in, but it wasn't from my friends. Janie wasn't great at texting, but she did send them on occasion, mostly if she needed to remind me of something, like a medication to give a horse or that one had to stay in for the farrier or vet or whatever.

Janie: New owners coming at 9. Please meet them and wait for me. Can't get there in time.

I eyed the screen. *Seriously?* She threw my entire world off course by not telling me she'd sold the farm or that Ava was leaving soon, and now she wanted me to entertain the people who were part of the problem?

Clenching my jaw, I tried to tamp down my annoyance. I wasn't entirely successful, so I just typed back: OK.

That gave me at least a half hour to stew in my frustration.

My phone vibrated.

Tessa: Aw, I'm so sorry! What happened?

Me: Gone this AM. Owners moved her yesterday. I didn't know!!!

Tessa: You weren't told???

Me: NO!!

Tessa: That's terrible.

Me: Don't even know where she went.

Tessa: Could you ask?

Me: Janie's being weird.

Tessa: She's losing her farm.

Me: She's the one who decided to sell it!!

Tessa: True, but we don't know why. Maybe she had to.

Me: I don't care!

Tessa: I'm sorry. It's not fair.

In the novels I read, the main character was supposed to be the star of the story. They were the one who *did* things and moved forward in life by their choices. I felt like a secondary character in my own story. Everything that was happening was happening *to* me. I had no choice about my dad's death, living with my aunt, Mom leaving me as a kid, Ava being taken away by her owners. But what if I could change that and take things into my own hands like Abraham had encouraged last night outside Tessa's? What if I decided to *do* something for a change?

Tessa: Are you okay?

I sighed. I wished Tessa were here in person because maybe her presence would calm me down a little. But she was probably either about to go to the pool or coming from the pool or thinking about the pool.

Me: Not entirely.

Tessa: Can you talk to your aunt?

Me: I did a little.

Tessa: I have swim lessons soon so have to run! Talk later?

Me: Yeah. Bye.

And just like that, it was almost nine o'clock.

Right on time, the couple I'd met earlier showed up in that giant truck, and I watched them from the barn doorway. If I was being truthful, I wanted to hate them. They were the reason Ava was gone. They were the reason I would lose the job I loved at Green Tree Farm.

They were also super friendly and nice.

"Hey there," Denise said. "Janie around?"

"She asked me to meet you," I said. "She's running late."

Brad joined his wife, and together they focused on me. I wanted to dissolve into the ground like a snowman melting in the July sun.

"I think maybe we got off on the wrong foot," Denise said with a smile. "Janie told us you hadn't known she was selling."

"No," I said, looking down at my boots. I struggled to make eye contact with people if I was nervous or feeling a lot of emotion.

Brad nodded. "That's rough."

"Yeah."

Stop sounding stupid, Shay. You do know how to speak in full sentences.

"Would you be up for showing us the barn?"

Anything would be better than standing around trying to make small talk. Small talk was not one of my gifts—it was about as bad as drama class.

Janie had said to wait for her, though I didn't think it mattered at this point *where* we waited. But hadn't they already seen the barn? I shrugged, then blushed at my teenage response. "Sure."

I walked down the barn aisle. Many of the horses were munching on their hay, and some were napping. I passed the stall of an older paint mare whose owner I'd never met. She was lying down sound asleep. Horses spend many hours a day resting, but they only sleep for two to three hours at most, and often that is broken up into smaller chunks.

"What's her name?" Denise paused outside the mare's stall.

"Sky." Sky's ear flicked at her name, and she hefted herself to her feet. She shook the bedding off her coat and stared at us.

Denise gestured toward her husband, and they seemed to share a moment of understanding as they watched the mare.

"There's something about her eyes," Denise said.

"Yeah. They're sad," I said. "She always looks that way." I rested my hand on the Dutch door, glancing at Ava's empty stall next to hers. "Makes sense. No one ever comes to see her."

"Well, there you go," Brad said.

Denise watched the mare for a second. "Horses get lonely too."

"She has four-legged friends," I said. "We turn the mares out together."

"That's good," Denise said.

I watched her face. She and Janie were probably similar in age, but Denise had a warmth about her I had to admit was nice.

"What's your story, old girl?" Denise's voice was soft, like she was talking to a sad kid.

Brad crossed his arms. "Sometimes horses connect with us humans in deep ways. We might not even realize it at first. Some horses couldn't care less about us; others enjoy our company like we enjoy theirs."

Denise nodded. "We had a horse once that came to us because his owner sold him when she went away to college. In his new home, he became a different horse, acting out all over the place.

Took us a while to realize he missed his owner. We had her come visit him, and it was incredible. He relaxed, let her saddle and ride him, and was the perfect boy."

I thought about Ava. At one point, her owners were going to sell her, and Janie had talked about buying her and starting a lesson program. What had happened to that idea? Now *Ava* was gone. Would she end up in some other home, missing her old friends?

"What happened to him?" I asked.

Denise smiled. "That college girl realized her horse needed her as much as she needed him and bought him back."

"If I had a horse, I would never sell it," I said.

"Sometimes life forces us to make choices we don't want to make," Brad said.

"I wouldn't sell it. Ever." I felt something start to rise in me—the fire of anger I'd worked so hard to manage in the past few months. I tried to focus on something else. We walked toward Chance's and Snow's stalls. Who would leave after them?

"When are you moving in?" I turned to face the couple, arms folded over my chest.

They gave each other looks again, like grown-ups often did. I hated that. I wasn't a kid anymore, and it made me feel like at any moment I'd get blindsided by something the grown-ups had known about for a long time and expected me to process in five minutes.

"Next week," Brad finally replied.

Chapter
15

Ironically, there were only three trees in the mare field at Green Tree Farm, but I found myself in their shade a few minutes later as I waited for Aunt Laura to pick me up. If I'd sat anywhere else, I would've roasted like a pig on a spit. But under the trees, I was at least sheltered from the sweltering sun. From my vantage point, I could see most of the farm.

I pulled my knees to my chest and stared at the empty field. Was it too much to want to stay here forever? When I started working at the farm, there was never a guarantee that I would stay or that it would become a full-time job. But it had become part of my life in ways I hadn't anticipated.

I had expected that an automatic perk of working at a barn would be the freedom to ride horses all I wanted, but it turned out those opportunities were few and far between since the boarders rode their own horses. Still, I got to be around the most amazing and beautiful creatures in the world. Living in town, with all its noise and signs and things demanding attention, could over-whelm me. Even the bookstore could be a cacophony of sounds and smells. But out here? I closed my eyes and listened. The only sounds were ones of nature. The rustling of the dry weeds the mower had missed along the fence line. A distant hawk calling from somewhere beyond my eyesight. Soon the buzzing of cicadas would punctuate this world.

If the horses were out here with me, I'd hear them blowing through their noses when a blade of grass tickled their whiskers or swishing their tails or stomping a hoof on the ground to ward off the relentless flies. Maybe I'd hear the jumbled hoofbeats as they all decided to be silly at the same time, racing around the pasture, bucking, tearing up and down the fence line—simply for fun or because they were startled by some imaginary terror. There was nothing in the world like watching horses run. Now I had lost my only opportunity to experience it all summer.

I opened my eyes and wiped my face. I was probably smudging dirt across my cheeks, but I didn't care.

Movement at the top of the pasture caught my eye. Someone was walking across the field toward me. I squinted to figure out who it was. In a moment, I knew. No one walked quite like our upbeat, positive-attitude Izzy.

I wondered why in the world she was here and why she hadn't texted me to let me know she was coming. And then I remembered. I had left my phone in the tack room by accident. I decided to stay in the shade and wait for her. She wore a straw sun hat, sunglasses with a blue tint, and a Captain America–shield sleeve-less T-shirt. But surprisingly, when she got closer, I could see that today she wore jeans tucked into . . . were those cowboy boots? I eyed her footwear, and she saw me do it.

"Do you like?" She struck a pose and giggled.

They were pink, spangled generously with rhinestones, and

stitched with turquoise thread. Definitely not *my* style, but most assuredly hers.

"They are so you," I said.

"Why, yes they are!" she said, admiring her boots again. She looked up at my smudged face. "Wait . . . were you crying?"

I took a deep breath. No use denying it. "Yeah."

Izzy plopped down beside me and gave me a one-armed hug. She wagged her feet, tapping the toes of her blingy boots together. "Aren't they cute? I look at them and instantly feel happy."

I smiled. Maybe a little bit of Izzy was what I needed. "*Cute* is the perfect word for them. How did you get here?" She and I both hadn't gotten our driver's licenses yet. Me out of fear, her out of convenience.

"Claire."

Claire was her older sister. "Doesn't she get tired of driving you around?"

"Nah. She loves to drive. Besides, she was going this way anyway." Izzy took off her sunglasses. "Shay. How are you? Really."

"Fine. I'm good."

"You sounded pretty upset in your texts," Izzy said, her voice quiet. She waved her hand around in the air. "And you've been crying." She crossed her legs and rested her forearms on them, the sunglasses hanging from her fingers. It was nice to talk in person and not through typing words on our phones.

"I'm sorry about your mom," Izzy said. Then she let the silence sit between us, not trying to explain things away or make me feel better.

I basked in the silent company for a few more moments. Sometimes all a girl needs is having someone who cares sit next to her. "It's okay," I said, starting to wave off her concern. But then I realized this was my chance to be real and maybe test the waters to deepen our friendship. I'd been somewhat vulnerable with my friends before—usually not on purpose—mostly when I was triggered by a burst of emotion. Tessa was probably the only one who had experienced the calm, vulnerable me when we'd spent time together last fall. Izzy's crazy energy, and the way she'd been bouncing around from hobby to hobby this summer, kind of made me wonder if she could go as deep as I needed right now.

"Well, that isn't quite true," I said. "It's not okay. I'm not okay. I don't even know what to feel, but I wish my grandmother had never told me."

"Do you know why she did?"

I shrugged. I realized it hadn't been all her doing. "She started talking about my mom, and I asked her to tell me more."

"Why didn't she tell you something nice?"

Good question.

"Maybe she wanted me to know the truth." I started pulling up little pieces of grass to keep my hands busy.

"The truth isn't always what we want to hear," Izzy said with a nod.

"Nope."

"I can't imagine how I'd feel if my mom did that."

"I didn't even know her, Izzy. But it still hurts."

"I bet you wish you could talk to your dad."

"Maybe he wouldn't have ever told me."

"It was probably super hard for him."

"I'm sure."

Izzy got quiet again, and I appreciated it. I wanted to ask her how she was doing lately, but I couldn't bring myself. I had nothing to give anyone else at the moment, and though I felt totally selfish about that, I couldn't seem to change it.

"The only thing I am sure of right now is that I'm not sure about anything." I'd thought my mother loved me, and then I found out she left. I thought God would protect someone like my dad and keep car accidents from happening. If He loved me like the Bible said, then why? I'd only recently, *finally* felt a semblance of normal in my life, and now that lay shattered on the floor of my heart.

Izzy nodded. "That's understandable, Shay."

"So . . . your boots." I nudged them with the toe of my much simpler, much dirtier pair.

Izzy sat up straighter. "They were on sale!"

And just like that, serious Izzy morphed into the girl I'd come to know and love—the girl who appreciated a good joke, who could bake and decorate cupcakes that looked like pieces of art-work, and who loved animals almost as much as I did.

"I was hoping, hoping, hoping," Izzy clasped her hands together as if begging, "to ride a horse today."

"What?"

"I know you said no last time, but couldn't it be now?"

"Izzy."

"It would be a dream come true."

"Now you're sounding like Amelia."

That made her laugh, then snort. "I am, aren't I?"

I climbed to my feet and brushed the dirt off my seat and legs. "I'm sorry. I've told you before that we can't ride a boarder's horse without their permission."

"Couldn't you ask them?"

"No."

"Why not?" She stood too, slipping her sunglasses back on. "Aren't they supposed to offer lessons here?"

Yeah, they were supposed to offer lessons. Same as they were supposed to keep the farm and not sell it. I wasn't sure what had abruptly changed for Janie, but clearly something had. And most of the horses were boarders whose owners were very picky about who rode their horse. I only knew a couple of them casually, and there was no way they'd let the stable girl get on and play.

"They're all going to be gone by next week."

Izzy spun toward me. "What?"

"Not like they can stay if the farm's sold."

"Couldn't they?"

"I wish." Not unless the new owners planned to keep this as a boarding stable, and it seemed that wasn't in their plans.

"Can we at least go brush them?" Izzy headed toward the barn, and I reluctantly followed. I didn't have the heart to tell her no again.

Together, we plodded up the hill.

"How are you doing about the"—*should I broach this subject?*—"whole Dropbox thing?"

For a second, it seemed like Izzy hadn't heard me. She didn't slow her pace and didn't respond.

"I mean, that had to be hard," I said.

"It was." Her words were quick.

"Just so you know, I believe you completely that you would never send anyone photos like that."

"Shay!" Izzy swung toward me with such speed that I flinched. "I would never!"

I held up my hands. "I know, I know! That's what I said!"

"I *wouldn't!*"

"I believe you. Amelia and Tessa do too. You know we all believe you, right?"

Now Izzy looked like she was about to cry, and I wished I'd kept my mouth shut. I hated this friendship thing. I wasn't good at it at all.

I waited for her to say something else, but she started walking away.

"Sorry, I was trying to—"

"I know. It's fine. I'm fine. I've given it to God. Zac moved away, so things are already much better." She smiled at me—a stiff, forced smile—then marched the rest of the way to the barn, and our moment of connecting was gone.

Chapter

16

Aunt Laura was going out to dinner with some old friends from her college days, so Stanley, Matilda, and I were alone in the apartment that evening. I didn't used to mind being alone. At least, I never minded when my dad was alive. Things changed after he died. I was still alone a lot because shyness will do that to you, but I didn't savor my solitude like before.

I didn't know what I'd done to offend Izzy, but she'd texted Claire shortly after she got to the barn, and her sister picked her up within the hour. Aunt Laura came for me around the same time.

"Frozen pizza?" my aunt suggested as she was leaving the apartment that evening.

I nodded and waved her off. My culinary skills weren't the best, but I could make a few easy things. It would be a whole lot more fun sharing the experience, like when Izzy made us lunch. I decided to be daring and do something spur-of-the-moment. I whipped out my phone.

Me: Hey! I'm making pizza. Anyone want to join me?

I fell onto the sofa with Stanley beside me and stared at my phone. If my friends were available, they would probably quickly text me back. Amelia and Izzy at least. Tessa sometimes took longer, as she was more like me and didn't consider her phone an appendage, but lately she'd gotten a lot faster, probably because she and her boyfriend, Alex, frequently communicated that way.

Nothing.

I stared at my blank phone, willing it to light up. Grams says, "A watched pot never boils." I guess a watched phone never pings.

I tried not to think about the barn being empty at Green Tree Farm next week, and me without a horsey place to go. But telling myself not to think about something only made me think about it more.

A text came in.

But it wasn't my friends.

Janie: Your last day will be next Weds. I'm sorry.

My heart kicked up. There it was. The finality I'd been dreading but hoping would somehow magically disappear. I had less than a week to figure out how I was going to handle it.

Me: OK.

What else was I supposed to say?

Janie: I'll pay you before I leave.

Me: Where are you going?

I didn't know Janie very well, even after working for her for several months. She kept our talk focused on horses, and when she went back to her house on the property, she did not want to be bothered.

Janie: Ohio

I hoped a little small talk would be acceptable, as I really did want to know.

Me: Family?

Janie: No.

Um . . . now what?

The right thing to do would be to wish her well, but I was still a little ticked at her for not telling me something sooner. I sighed. *It's not like everyone has to share their personal business with you, Shay.*

Me: **Hope things go well.**

That was pretty lame, but at least it was something.

A text finally came into my friends' thread.

Tessa: **Sorry, can't tonight! Babysitting Logan.**

Me: **Ok, have fun!**

Amelia: **Theater camp stuff tonight!!!! Gotta prep.**

Me: **Gotcha!**

I stared at my screen and waited for Izzy, but she wasn't going to respond. I'd obviously upset her today, and even though she wasn't the type to be passive-aggressive, I probably wouldn't be able to mend this in a night.

I hadn't realized how much I'd let myself get excited about the spontaneity of having even one of my friends come to cook something together again. Although we all texted almost every day, and I'd seen Izzy this morning, I felt alone.

I popped the pizza in the oven. Sometimes I felt like I was the only one in our group who was completely alone. Izzy had her cozy family. Tessa had her little brother, her swim gang, and her mom. Amelia reveled in her theater people like a queen bee in a hive. People were drawn to her. I sort of had my aunt. But it was still new for us.

I decided to text her: **Hope you have fun tonight!**

Because you'll have to have fun for both of us.

I spent twenty minutes throwing myself a grand pity party as I waited for the pizza to finish cooking. When it did, I cut it into four huge pieces and placed two of them on my plate. I reached for my phone with the intention of scrolling through Instagram. In the past, I would've been much more likely to pick up a book while I ate. But lately, I hadn't found a book that captured my attention.

I kept pulling books from the shelves, reading one chapter, and then putting them back, only to take another and find that it wasn't capturing me either.

Except one.

The pizza was scalding, so I set it aside on the counter while I went to get the book from underneath my bed, hoping Stanley still hadn't learned the art of counter surfing.

I set the book and the pizza on the kitchen table. I grabbed three napkins and sat. I took my first bite and stared at the cover, remembering what that first chapter had described. With no one around to question me, my embarrassment faded, and my curiosity grew.

If Tessa saw me ready to open this book, she would tell me to throw it away. I could pretty much see her crinkling her nose in disgust. But . . . I pulled it closer. Tessa wasn't here. I'd wanted her to be, but she was too busy. Was that my fault?

In what felt like an act of defiance, I opened the novel to the next chapter and started reading while I ate. Some of the story was normal, with a plot that seemed to make sense, but I hadn't finished the fourth chapter before I came to another scene that could've been describing what was on the cover. Before I knew it, I'd finished my pizza and was devouring more chapters in equal parts fascination and horror. My dad had raised me to believe that sex should be treasured and only experienced between a husband and wife. This author clearly did not hold those views. Not that I expected a book with that kind of cover to practice what the Bible taught.

I kept turning the pages. I wanted to stop because part of it was gross. But it was also fascinating. My imagination created vivid pictures of what was going on in the story. When I was reading that book, I wasn't thinking about anything else. It filled my mind so much that everything else—all the sadness, loneliness, and loss—faded.

Chapter
17

My phone rang. It startled me so much I nearly dropped the book on the sofa where I'd moved to be more comfortable. I was so used to texting and video chatting that talking to someone on the phone had become foreign.

Grams.

Oh man. I was not in the mood to talk to her, but I was already feeling guilty about what I was reading. I didn't want to add guilt upon guilt.

"Hello?"

"Shay."

I tried to guess from her tone how the conversation was going to go. At least it didn't sound like she was calling to report a disaster.

"Hey, Grams."

"Have you considered coming with us to the cottage? We would like to spend some time with you."

"Uh . . ."

It took me a second to switch gears. My mind was still in the
world of the novel, and I felt myself flush in shame at the thought
of Grams knowing. She was the type of grandmother who would
have scolded me if I even suggested watching a movie that wasn't
rated G or PG.

"A lot's been going on," I said.

"Summer will be over before you know it."

I didn't like to think about that. I had at least another month,
right?

"Grams, why did you hate my mom so much? Was she really
such an awful person?"

Whoa. I surprised myself with my boldness, but I was tired of
the unknown and didn't want to beat around the bush. My grandmother was silent for a moment—a feat for her.

"I did not hate her," Grams replied.

"Could've fooled me."

The heat I'd felt along my neck a few minutes earlier increased,
not from embarrassment but from a very familiar anger that I'd
done my best to tamp down these past few months. I wasn't sure if
it was because I couldn't see my grandmother and the only things
connecting us were some floating sound waves, or because everything I'd kept inside was surfacing. Either way, I wanted to say
things that, even in the heated moment, I shouldn't.

"They loved each other," I said, poking my finger in the air to
emphasize it. "I don't care what you say. They did."

"Your father was . . . blinded by it."

"That's not true!"

"You were a child. A baby."

"He loved her. That matters."

That caused my grandmother to laugh. "You are so naive,
Shay."

Her words cut, and my feelings bled. "I'm more perceptive than
you think." I jutted my chin out as if my grandmother could see me.

"In some ways."

"He never said one bad thing about her," I said.

"And why would he?" Grams softened her voice in the way I hated—talking to me as if I were five years old.

"Because he always told me the truth. And he loved me," I said.

"Love causes people to do foolish things."

I understood Grams was now talking about a whole lot more than me or my mother or even her son, but it was hard to hang on to that when all I really longed to hear was that she believed in me at least a little bit. If she were to show any signs of that, I felt like I could accept what she was saying a whole lot more. If I knew *she* truly loved *me*, then maybe it wouldn't be so hard to believe she was just trying to help me understand my family.

The lock in the apartment door clicked, and Stanley lifted his head from the couch.

"I better go," I said to Grams, and without waiting for a reply, tapped to end the call.

Aunt Laura walked through the door. As Stanley jumped off to greet her, I scooped up the novel, held the front of the book against me so my aunt wouldn't see the cover, and dashed to my room.

"Hi," Aunt Laura called after me.

"Hey," I said, glancing over my shoulder.

My aunt was holding a box with handles and set it on the ground. "I have something for you."

"Be right back."

I went to my bed and tucked the book in its hiding spot. My heart pounded. Kneeling beside the bed, I tried to calm myself. If what I was doing wasn't wrong, why was I afraid for my aunt to see? For anyone to see?

God, I'm sorry, I whispered.

And I was. I really was.

Holding my head in my hands, I tried to breathe. Why couldn't one conversation with Grams ever go right?

I found my aunt in the kitchen, making herself a cup of coffee. She could drink the stuff before bed and still fall asleep.

"You doing okay?" she asked, stirring hazelnut creamer into her coffee.

"Yeah."

Aunt Laura eyed me. "You're a horrible liar."

"I'm not lying."

"Shay."

"I don't lie!" I lied.

"I'm teasing, kiddo."

"It isn't funny."

"Okay, I see that."

I was *not* doing okay, thank you very much. But it wasn't as if something terrible had happened. What right did I have to be so upset over normal, simple life things? After Dad died, I'd wished for an ordinary life. I longed to go back and experience the mundane things I'd thought were boring before. As each month passed afterward, I longed for it even more.

"Summer's almost over," I said, dropping into a kitchen chair.

My aunt sat across from me. "You still have weeks. Don't get mopey yet."

"I thought I was going to be at the barn forever."

Aunt Laura smiled, taking a sip from her coffee. "Forever?"

"Almost forever."

She raised an eyebrow.

"I just can't believe it's going to be gone."

"Now hold on. You've met the new owners, right?"

"Yeah."

"And they seem nice."

"I guess."

"Shay, you never know what's going to happen."

"All the horses are leaving. They're my friends."

"I know, I know. Your mom was like that too."

Stanley came and rested his head in my lap, and I started rubbing his ears. "How so?"

"Oh my gosh, didn't I tell you about what she was like growing up?"

She had a little, but I needed to hear it again.

"She'd yell at our parents if they didn't slow down for a squirrel in the road. Or an escaped chicken. Everywhere she went, animals were drawn to her. Even our family dog adopted her as his favorite person. It was uncanny," Aunt Laura said. "You have the same gift."

"She left us," I whispered, my voice still catching.

"I know. But her leaving doesn't mean she wasn't a good person with a good heart. She just made some really stupid decisions."

I sniffed. "So I'm like her in that way too."

When I first arrived in Riverbend, I had tried to hide the fact that I'd been in juvie for a month because I'd punched a girl for talking smack about my parents. Eventually, I told my friends, and then the whole school found out.

From then on, I was always trying to be good and do the right thing, be the right person. Probably in part to try to make up for those mistakes. Certainly, I didn't want to ever be in that place of shame and mortification again.

"Remember, Shay, you aren't your parents." Aunt Laura took another sip of her coffee. "You get to live your own life and make your own choices."

Yeah, and I was doing great in that department.

"Making your own choices doesn't mean you're going to be perfect, okay?" Aunt Laura said, as if she could read my thoughts. "Mistakes are allowed. That's called life. Hopefully we learn from those mistakes. It almost makes them worth it." She grinned big.

"I wish I *was* perfect," I muttered.

That caused Aunt Laura to laugh. "Oh, kid."

"I do," I said.

"And I wish I was queen of England, but both are impossible."

"Okay." I rolled my eyes.

"Quit trying to be perfect. Figure out who *you* are and be that. You'll have a much better chance of succeeding." She got up, went over to the box on the living room floor, and tapped on the lid. "Come here. I have something to show you."

Chapter
18

HUMANS AND HORSES have a huge curiosity gene that gets the better of us sometimes. I perked up at my aunt's words.

"When your dad died, your grandmother let me keep a few of his things."

Aunt Laura removed the lid and set it on the floor. Stanley immediately started sniffing the lid and pushing it around with his nose.

My pulse kicked up a notch. I wasn't sure if I was ready for something like this, yet I couldn't keep myself from moving closer.

"I think this is the right time to give them to you," my aunt said.

Do not cry, do not cry, do not cry.

Aunt Laura smiled. "I wanted to make sure you had something tangible to remember him by."

Okay, now she was going to make me cry. I wanted to hug her but wasn't sure if I would completely break down if I did.

"You can look at them now, or later, or never." Aunt Laura slid the box over to me. "It's not much, but it's something."

I hesitated, feeling my hand tremble. "Thank you."

"You're very welcome."

Why was I scared to see what was inside?

I swallowed. "Will you go through it with me?"

"You bet."

We sat on opposite sides of the box and slowly pulled out each item. The first thing my hand touched was Dad's leather wallet. It was falling apart, the old carving almost worn smooth, the lacing along the edge half missing.

"He made that when he was a kid," I said.

"Pretty sentimental guy if he used it his whole life," Aunt Laura said with a chuckle.

In the wallet was Dad's driver's license, insurance cards, credit cards, a business card for a dry cleaner, and a photo of me. I slipped it out.

"You were a cutie," Aunt Laura said.

I groaned. "Look at how chubby I was."

"Oh, you were not."

My little puffy cheeks said otherwise, but I stared at the photo. Because I'd done cyber school, I didn't have official school pics like some kids. But Dad still took photos of me every year, posed as though I were going to school. I was probably eight years old in this photo. I think it was taken at the reservoir, and I'd been focused on the flock of geese only a few feet away.

I took out a crinkled note tucked inside the wallet. I unfolded it and read the note written in a child's scrawl. Mine. *I luv you, Daddy!* I'd drawn a picture of what I meant to be a horse but looked like a big circle with legs.

I showed my aunt, and she laughed.

"Not exactly Rembrandt," I said.

"Come on. You were little."

"I still can't draw!"

We both laughed then, and it felt good.

A faded Post-it Note was also stuck in the wallet. In my dad's handwriting was the verse *He who is in you is greater than he who is in the world. — 1 John 4:4*. I showed it to Aunt Laura.

"Wonder why he picked that one," I said.

She shrugged.

The next thing I found was a portable hard drive. Dad had placed a strip of duct tape on it and written *Book Covers* on the tape.

"I didn't look at the files," Aunt Laura said. "But I think he kept digital copies of all his covers."

"*All* of them?"

"You'll have to see."

Also in the box was Dad's worn Bible. I wasn't sure why, but a wave of guilt washed over me. My father hadn't read his Bible every day, or even gone to church every week, but he tried. His faith had meant something to him.

I opened it and carefully thumbed through the pages. Many of them had verses underlined with notes in the margins. I skimmed through a few and decided I wanted to look more carefully later. I set the Bible aside and took out a stack of birthday cards with a rubber band keeping them together. Many of them were from me, my handwriting getting a little better with each card.

Aunt Laura handed over a fountain pen he'd kept on his desk and a striped, rust-colored feather.

I held the feather up to my aunt.

"I don't know why I took that," she said. "I figured it must mean something that no one would know but you."

"We found it camping one year." I twirled it in my fingers. "Dad said it was from a red-tailed hawk. He told me some Native Americans believed it symbolized we were exactly where we should be in life."

I thought of my recent texts with the girls and how I'd expressed my doubts about God and life and being where I should be. My dad would've probably agreed with their answers—trusting God even when it seemed hard or when things didn't make sense.

There were a few other things I couldn't look at without getting emotional. A flannel shirt he had worn a lot that still smelled like his cologne, and his favorite watch a buddy had given him for his birthday one year.

The last thing in the box was another box, this one metal with a four-number combination.

I glanced at my aunt.

"I have no idea how to unlock that," Aunt Laura said. "I tried all kinds of combinations."

I lifted the box and shook it. Felt like something was in there for sure. Without thinking, I adjusted the numbers to 6590.

The lid opened.

"How did—?"

"The street number on our house. We used it for all sorts of stuff."

Aunt Laura threw up her hands. "I never would have guessed that one."

Inside was a single item. A gray journal. I opened it. The first date was almost twenty years ago. I turned it toward Aunt Laura, and she held out her hand. I gave her the journal. She paged through it, then slowly set it back down on the table with a long sigh.

I stared at the book. "What?"

"I don't know that either of us are ready for this."

I looked over all the items littering the table, the only tangible reminders I had of my dad, and wondered if this was going to be one of those moments that changed everything. That meant I could never go back to the way I was before.

"I'd recognize that handwriting anywhere, Shay." Aunt Laura ran her hands through her hair. "It's your mom's."

Chapter
19

"Are you serious?" I picked up the journal like it was a baby animal—gingerly, as if I might hurt it. Was I about to get the answers I'd been needing ever since my grandmother told me about Mom? Scratch that. The answers I'd been needing my whole *life*.

"I can't believe it's hers," Aunt Laura said, staring at the book in my hands.

I realized my aunt might want this journal for herself. My mom was her sister, and she hadn't exactly gotten much closure either.

"This is yours," I said, holding it out to her.

She shook her head. "I think you need to have it. I'll read it later if you're okay with that."

I nodded. I didn't know what I would find, but that seemed fair.

We packed the other stuff back into the box. "Thank you," I said.

"I know things have been rough." Aunt Laura placed the lid

back on the box and slid it across the floor to me. "Hopefully this helps a little."

I smiled, but I wasn't quite sure if it was real or if my aunt even noticed.

Later that night, I settled into my pillow and held the journal to my chest. Stanley had jumped onto the bed with me and lay sprawled, taking up half the mattress and pushing his long legs against me. Sometimes in the middle of the night, I'd end up huddled on a sliver of the bed while he kicked me in his sleep.

I pulled out my phone and zapped a text to the girls.

Me: Aunt Laura gave me a journal of my mom's.

A minute later Tessa replied: That's so cool!

Me: I think it is?

Tessa: Why wouldn't it be?

Me: Um, I haven't read it yet.

Tessa: What are you waiting for?

Should I tell her I was scared out of my mind over what I would find? Logic told me this journal wasn't going to be all happy thoughts. And I didn't want it to be, right? The truth wasn't always pretty. I'd certainly learned that in the past couple of months, but the little girl in me also wanted to know Mom wasn't a complete nut job.

Okay, maybe I *did* want it to be all happy thoughts.

Me: Not sure what I'll find.

Tessa: Only one way to know! ☺

Me: U used an emoji!!!

Tessa: LOL. I guess I did!

Me: Is this really Tessa? Or did someone hijack your phone?

Tessa: Ha ha. For real. You doing okay?

Me: I guess I'll let you know when I read it.

Tessa: Do you want me to come over?

I paused. Glanced at my clock. It was early still, only nine fifteen. Was she serious?

Me: It's late.

Tessa: I'll come if you need me to.

My heart warmed at her offer. Even though all of us were super busy this summer, we still cared about each other. Izzy would come around, and we'd still be friends. Amelia would probably realize someday that there was more to life than theater, and maybe I would be okay not working at a barn.

Tessa: I'll be there in five minutes.

Darn it, Tessa, don't be so nice to me or else I'm going to cry.

I started typing a protest, but then stopped. Why wouldn't I let her be there for me? Would that be such a bad thing? I pressed the delete button.

Me: OK. Thank you.

I quickly checked with Aunt Laura to make sure she was cool with the idea, and then I waited on the sofa with Stanley. Within a few minutes, a knock came on our back door—the outside entrance to our apartment.

Tessa walked in and gave me a quick hug. I wanted to hang on to her, but I let her go.

"So, where is it?" she said, smiling.

She was dressed in a T-shirt and gym shorts, and she patted Stanley on the head when he came over to her, his tail wagging. She wasn't as animal crazy as me or Izzy, but Stanley liked her, and dogs were good judges of character.

"You didn't have to come," I said.

"I know."

I wanted to tell her I was glad she did, but I couldn't quite bring the words to my lips.

"Have fun, girls," Aunt Laura said from her desk in the corner. My bedroom used to be her office, but she'd moved her stuff into the living room when I moved in. I still felt a little bad about that, but what were our options?

We plopped onto my bed, and Tessa sat crisscross, leaning back on her hands. I held out the journal for her to take.

"Really?" she said, not moving.

"I can't bring myself to start."

"You can do it."

"I can't."

She must have realized the strength of my feelings because she shifted position, gently took the journal, and opened it up to the first page.

"Out loud?"

I gave a small nod.

Tessa cleared her throat. "First entry is from eighteen years ago."

"Okay, approximately two years before I was born."

"Here goes."

Tessa began to read, then started laughing.

"What?"

She pointed at the journal. "Oh my gosh, Shay."

"What is it?"

Tessa took on a mock serious tone and read, *"I met a cute dog today."*

"No way! She wrote that?"

"Yes!"

My friend turned the journal toward me. There it was. In blue ink.

"Some girls talk about boys, but no. Shay and Jessica Mitchell are all about the dogs," Tessa said.

"Hear that, Stanley?" I hung over the side of the bed to where the greyhound napped in his cave bed.

Tessa kept going, and Mom described meeting a neighbor's dog. The next few entries were pretty fluffy too, talking about her job waitressing and how she was struggling to pay off her student loans.

"Each entry seems to be written with a different pen," Tessa said. "Blue ink here, purple there. And sometimes ballpoint, other times not. Here's one in pencil." Tessa turned the journal toward me. I started to read the entry and felt myself tense.

"I took the test. I'm pregnant."

"Hey, that's you!" Tessa said. "She's pregnant with you."

"Yeah."

"Shay, this is good. You wanted this."

"Can I change my mind now?"

Tessa playfully smacked my arm. "Read!"

I swallowed. My tongue seemed to have dried up. Why is it that when the things we want the most get within reach, we sometimes decide that maybe we don't want them after all? Expectations can be cruel. What seemed so exciting, intriguing, and wonderful doesn't always live up to our fertile imaginations. *Look what happened when I asked Grams about Mom.*

When I'd first handed Tessa the journal, I had no idea what my expectations were. I only knew I didn't want to be shocked by anything.

"Shay, it's okay."

I rolled onto my back and continued reading out loud. *"I've only told Laura, and she freaked."* I rested the book on my chest. "Freaked?"

"I probably would too," Tessa said.

I kept reading. *"I don't know if I'll tell Mason or not."*

Mason King. My biological father, the famous horse trainer.

Tessa tapped her foot on the bed. "She didn't, right?"

"Not that I know of."

"Keep reading."

"I'm trying, but someone keeps interrupting me!"

Tessa laughed.

The journal went on, "*I feel so many things, but I think the biggest thing of all is that I don't know if I'm ready to . . . be a mom.*"

Right then, Tessa's phone rang, and when she reached to grab it, she accidentally pushed it off the edge of the bed. I heard it *thud* on the wood floor. Normally I would've been all about helping Tessa retrieve her phone, but all I could do was stare at the page of my mom's cursive handwriting as my friend climbed off the bed.

I made myself breathe in and out. *Okay, she'd just found out she was pregnant. A lot of women would have this reaction even when they wanted kids, right? They wouldn't think they were prepared or capable or a whole host of other feelings.*

I read the next few lines silently to myself: *Laura thinks I should tell Mason, but I don't know. He doesn't want kids either.*

Either?

I closed the journal. I knew this was going to be hard, but couldn't I catch one break?

Tessa climbed back onto the bed, cell phone in hand. "Spam call," she said. She had a weird look on her face I couldn't figure out, but it probably matched mine.

"What if she never wanted to have me?"

"But she did," Tessa said, the weird look fading. "You've got to remember that. Maybe not at first, but you're here today because your mom gave birth to you. That's huge. She wasn't married, sounds like the guy wasn't in the picture, and yet she still had you."

"I don't know if I can read the rest."

Tessa gave me an encouraging smile. "Then don't. But now you have the option. You didn't have that before."

I grabbed the journal again, wiping my hand across the plain cover. My mother had held this book. Her fingerprints might even still be on it. I was so thankful to finally have a peek into her head, but I was also scared about what else I would find.

"I'm gonna call it a night," I said, tucking the journal into my nightstand. The rest of it would have to wait until later.

Tessa stayed with me for a few more minutes, then left for home. When I was alone again in the darkness of my bedroom, my dog lying beside me, my aunt still awake in the living room, I brought up my e-mail on my phone and opened the Drafts folder. I clicked on the most recent e-mail I'd written a few days ago.

Dear Mason King . . . the short e-mail began.

I almost tapped the send icon. My mom hadn't been able to tell this man she was having his child. How different would my life be if she had? My finger hovered over the phone. I could change everything right now. I yearned for family. What if Mason King was the key to that?

Chapter
20

I SENSED SOMETHING WAS DIFFERENT the moment I walked into the barn the next morning. Janie already had the horses inside and was busy filling hay nets, something I normally did.

"What should I do?" I asked.

Janie barely acknowledged me. "Waters."

Each stall had a water spigot with a short hose attached. That made it easier to top off the water buckets in the morning. Several horses liked to dunk their hay in their buckets before they ate it, so I'd have to pull hay out too. At least once a week, we removed the buckets and washed them out thoroughly.

Fourteen horses had dwindled to ten, and tomorrow was my last day.

I did the remaining chores in less than an hour, right before the first horse trailer showed up. I didn't want to ask who was leaving, but I did anyway.

"Six today," Janie said and told me their names.

My stomach clenched.

"Have you heard from Ava's owners?"

"Nope."

I tried to get a good look at Janie. She was going through a tack trunk and tossing smooshed brushes and old, ratty saddle pads into the garbage can. I never did learn the story of why she bought the farm in the first place, or why she was selling it now. Even though this loss was hard for me, it had to be much harder for her.

A horse softly nickered behind me, and I turned toward Sky, the paint mare. She was staring right at me.

"Hey, girl." I went over to her stall and gently touched her soft, pink nose. "When is she leaving?" I asked Janie.

The older woman looked up, a faded, threadbare saddle blanket in her hand. "I don't know. Owners haven't responded to me. They also didn't pay board last month."

"I can't believe it."

Janie shrugged. "Happens."

"What if they don't come for her?"

"You ask too many questions, Shay."

I didn't think my questions were all that unreasonable, but . . .

"You can go home now," Janie said. "Probably won't need your help tomorrow either."

"I can come anyway."

"I said we won't need your help."

"But I had until Wednesday."

"Pay's in an envelope in the tack room."

I stood there in the barn aisle, my emotions bubbling. It disturbed me that, once again, anger was the emotion quickly rising to the top. But this time I saw it like I was outside myself. I felt every ounce of that anger . . . and decided to choose a different path.

"I've worked my butt off for you here," I said. My tone wasn't mean, but I needed to be honest.

"Yeah?" Janie pulled out a moldy bridle and tossed it in the trash with a clatter. "You oughta be glad I even let you on this place—rookie mistakes left and right, keeping things as tidy as a slob. You're lucky I didn't fire you the first month."

Whoa. I inched closer to Sky. Where was *that* coming from?

"You ungrateful little girls think you can come waltzing into a barn, work a few hours, and go gallivanting around on the horses like you're Olympic hopefuls." Janie stood up with a wince, probably from her bum knee. Her voice was rising in pitch. "Well, it doesn't work that way. Horses are hard work, and they'll eat you out of house and home. And at the end of the day, you'll have nothing to show for it."

"I am grateful," I said.

"You get too attached and soft, and they'll break your heart and toss you to the ground like a sack of feed. You can't let 'em do that. You'll never be able to survive in the horse business."

I was now pretty sure she wasn't talking about me, but her words hurt nonetheless. I really had given 100 percent to this little barn job.

Janie grabbed a handful of tangled polo wraps and started to unwind them, but they were twisted together in a knot, and she slammed the whole bundle into the trash can. "Horses aren't worth it," she grumbled. "Sooner you learn that, the better."

"They are worth it," I said.

Janie shook her head. "You're young and naive."

Naive. The same word Grams used to describe me.

Before I could figure out how to respond, two more trucks towing trailers arrived, and Janie focused on them. I didn't interact with a lot of the owners, so the people who quickly filled the barn were practically strangers. I felt about as important as the dirt on the toe of my boot.

I stepped outside and regretted it. The sun beat down. The cicadas buzzed in the trees like an Indiana summer's insect siren announcing you'd better be prepared to sweat.

A horse's whinny pierced the air, and I wanted to hold my hands over my ears. Changing barns would be upsetting to any of them. They were leaving their friends, their familiar surroundings, everything. I remembered what it felt like to move to Riverbend. My life had been upended, and it took me a long time to start finding my way—and nearly a year later, I still hadn't completely found my footing.

Hooves banged against metal as one of the horses was loaded onto the trailer at the other end of the barn. I knew if I watched, I'd start bawling. As it was, my chest felt constricted, and it was hard to breathe deeply.

"Hey, give me a hand with this?"

I looked up to see an older man with nearly white hair, a moustache, and bushy eyebrows that looked like chunks of steel wool glued to his forehead. He was unloading a tack trunk from the back of an old pickup.

I pointed at myself. "Me?"

"Look like anyone else is around? Yes, you."

Um, okay.

I reluctantly grabbed one handle on the trunk. The man grabbed the other.

"Where are we going?" I asked.

"Where do you think?"

It looked like the barn was exchanging one cranky old person for another, though this guy was much older than Janie, probably in his seventies. His jeans were dirtier than mine, and the leather of his boots was cracked. He wore a short-sleeved plaid shirt with the top two buttons undone, the wrinkled, tan skin of his neck giving away that he was probably a real farm guy and not one of the fake ones who came through on the arms of their horse-loving girlfriends.

I was trying to figure out who this guy was if he was bringing a trunk *in* rather than *out*. He must be part of Brad and Denise's crew. But asking "Who are you?" when I wasn't even supposed to be around seemed odd.

"You the kid who works here?"

What was *in* this trunk? It felt like a load of bricks.

I huffed in air, trying to keep up with the guy as we walked the trunk through the aisle and into the tack room. Half the stuff in the room was still there, but an area in the corner had been cleared.

"I *did* work here," I said.

"Want to stay on?"

I looked at him, uncomprehending. Surely he hadn't said what I thought he said. So I didn't answer.

The old man nodded toward the corner, and I shuffled over there. The man wasn't even breathing hard when he set his corner of the trunk down. I did the same with mine and felt sweat beading on my forehead.

I started to walk away, but the man held out his hand.

"Link," he said.

I reluctantly shook it, feeling all the hard calluses on his palm—more proof he was the real deal.

"That's a weird name," I said before I could stop the words from popping out my mouth. "I mean, it's a name I haven't heard before, and I . . ." My voice trailed off.

The man chuckled.

I felt my cheeks turn even redder than they already were from the heat.

"Yours?" he asked.

"Shay."

He laughed. "You think *my* name's weird?"

My first feeling was a twinge of offense. His wide grin made me think I was supposed to laugh too. I guess I was the one who started it.

"You wanna work here or not?"

"Who are you again?" I eyed him the way Stanley did when we offered him a treat with medicine stuffed in the middle.

"Fair enough," Link said, turning and walking out of the tack room like I was supposed to follow.

"I'm the barn manager at Second Chance Farm." Link walked over to his truck and started pulling another trunk from the bed. "Today's movin'-in day."

"I kind of figured that," I said, then realized that sounded snarkier than I intended. "Sorry," I added.

"Grab the trunk, Miss Shay." Link pulled the scratched wooden box to the edge of the truck bed and pointed at it. "That is, if you want to stay."

One of the trucks and trailers slowly pulled onto the long driveway of Green Tree Farm, the horse inside the box kicking the sides of the trailer. In some ways, a part of my life was leaving today, never to return. As I reached for the side of the trunk closest to me, I thought that maybe, just maybe, something else was beginning.

Chapter
21

"Whoa," Aunt Laura said when I climbed into the car. "Is that a smile?"

"Ha. Ha."

"What happened?"

We pulled onto the road behind the second horse trailer of the day, the one with two horses on board. A gelding and a mare, both chestnuts with white stars on their foreheads. Only way I could tell them apart was to look underneath for their boy or girl parts.

My heart followed the trailer as it turned in the opposite direction from us. Two more friends I'd probably never see again.

"And there it went," Aunt Laura said.

I focused back on her. "Sorry."

"It's been a rough time for you. I get it."

I told my aunt about the new barn manager and being asked to stay.

"That's great news, Shay!"

"I guess."

"You don't think so?"

"Well, yeah, but . . ." How could I explain my weird mix of thoughts and emotions? Of course it was a good thing. It was a *great* thing. I'd still have horses in my life. I should be jumping up and down, texting my friends the great news and saying the expected "Thank you, Jesus!" So why wasn't I?

"But?" Aunt Laura said.

I had never liked change, even before my dad was killed in the car accident. And now I was tired of radical changes. I was tired of my life being turned inside out, of being tossed around by the choices of the adults in charge of me. Tired of nothing being steady and the same. Was it too much to ask for at least one thing to remain constant?

"I'm glad," I said. "Really glad I get to keep working at the barn. But they won't be the same horses. I'm going to miss Ava and Chance and Snow." And every other horse I'd come to love. "And I guess I'm hesitant to get too excited because I don't know what these new owners will be like to work for. What if they're mean to me—or worse, to the horses?"

"If they are, we'll deal with that when it comes. If you think about it, the future is never certain. And it wouldn't be even if Janie stayed. The owners could move their horses at any moment."

She was right, of course. But deep inside, I still felt the loss of what I had at Green Tree Farm.

Aunt Laura got quiet for a minute, and I let the silence spread through the Jeep. I was glad she was okay with silence. She sometimes got lost in her own thoughts and wouldn't even hear me if I asked her a question. But by the way she kept glancing at me, I was pretty sure she wanted to speak but wasn't sure she should.

"What?" I asked.

My aunt chuckled a little. "It's that obvious?"

"Um, yeah."

"You don't have to tell me, but did you read any of the journal?"

Oh.

I wasn't sure if I was ready for *that* conversation.

"Some," I said.

Aunt Laura was not going to pry, I could tell. But she did deserve something since it was her sister's, and she was the one who had so kindly given it to me.

"A few things are hard to read," I said. "She talked about telling you she was pregnant."

My aunt sighed. "I remember that day so well."

"Were you mad at her?"

Aunt Laura's forehead wrinkled. "A little."

"Why?"

"I shouldn't have been. She needed me to support her."

"Didn't you?"

That was probably an unfair question. By the way my aunt stared straight ahead down the road, I could tell she was struggling to respond.

"It wasn't that I didn't want her to have you. You need to know that for sure." Aunt Laura turned and looked directly into my eyes. "Okay?"

I nodded but glanced away.

"She was my big sister, and I looked up to her."

I could only imagine what having a sibling felt like. Maybe it would be like having Tessa as a sister instead of as a friend. Or even Zoe, if we were talking a much older sibling like Mom was to Aunt Laura.

"We were raised a certain way, with certain expectations and ways to live life. Set values. Your mom kind of threw those away when she was in college."

I instantly thought about the book under my bed and the graphic scenes I'd read and kept reading. Was I like my mom? When I turned eighteen, what would keep me from moving out and doing things completely different from the way my dad had raised me or the values Aunt Laura was trying to encourage me toward? Hadn't I already begun down that path my mom had walked? I didn't read my Bible much anymore. I went to church only when my friends begged me or Aunt Laura made me. I knew those things didn't change whether I was a Christian, but didn't they show where my heart was?

I could feel the frustration rising in me, and I shoved it back down as hard as I could.

"I was pretty young, too," Aunt Laura said. "I'd do things differently now. Respond differently."

We rode the rest of the way back home in contemplative silence. When Aunt Laura parked, she asked me if I could help her in the bookstore.

"The fiction section needs to be alphabetized again," she said. "Some kids mixed things up, probably on purpose, thinking it was funny."

An hour later, I found myself in the romance section again, and my heart began to beat a little faster as I worked. I wanted to get my job done well and not take the entire day to do it, but what was the point of working in a bookstore if you couldn't stop to open a book every once in a while?

I pulled out another title, the cover igniting a flush. I quickly glanced around to see if anyone was watching me. A couple customers, several shelves over, were focused on the books in their hands. They wouldn't care.

Why am I doing this?

Things were going okay. I might not be losing the barn like I thought, and my aunt cared about me and wanted to talk. She wasn't an adult who ignored me and got sucked into her own life. My friends might be busy, but they did care. I didn't need to do this to distract myself.

My self-talk didn't do a thing. I kept reading anyway. Even

as that little voice kept whispering for me to do the right thing, another one clamored for attention, like a mustang rearing into the air in defiance. *Listen to me! You know that ordinary life you keep wishing for? It's never going to happen. That family you long for is gone forever. You're going to disappoint your grandmother no matter what you say or do, so why not do what you want? Go ahead and contact Mason King too! It doesn't matter if he was hurting Ava. He probably didn't mean to. You're missing out on so much.*

"What are you doing?"

I literally jumped, nearly dropping the book.

I hadn't noticed Tessa standing beside me any more than I had the other day.

"We've been trying to get your attention."

I swallowed hard. My face was hot, and I quickly closed the book and reshelved it, walking as fast as I could toward the alcove with the beanbag chairs and sofa my friends and I usually commandeered.

"That must've been an amazing book," Amelia said, falling back onto the yellow beanbag chair, an issue of *American Theatre* in hand. I think my aunt special ordered the magazine for her.

"Technically, I'm working," I said to the girls. I couldn't look at any of them. Especially Izzy, who still wasn't texting me like she had before.

"Can you hang out when you're done?" Amelia asked, barely looking up from the magazine.

"I'm not sure."

Tessa was giving me a look. "We should talk," she said.

I'd been pining to spend more time with my friends for how many weeks now, and here they all were in front of me, and *I* was the one making excuses? I knew full well I could ask my aunt if I could finish later, and I suspected at least Tessa knew it too.

Izzy lounged in the other chair, holding a cookbook called

The Perfect Cake. She lowered it to give me a good stare. Then she smiled at me. It wasn't big, but it was real. I tried to smile back.

"Come on, Shay," Izzy said. "We want to hang with you."

It was all I could do not to run away like that imaginary mustang. Izzy said that now, but what if she knew about the thoughts running through my head? Because the thing I feared the most was worse even than losing the horses.

I feared my friends running away from *me*.

Chapter
22

"We should get ice cream." Amelia sighed and closed her eyes, resting her hands behind her head. "I dream of chocolate decadence with peanut butter swirls and—"

"Yes!" Izzy snapped her cookbook shut. "Or caramel ripples loaded with Oreo pieces."

"Stop it, you guys!" I tried to infuse as much goofiness into my voice as I could. I needed them to think I was perfectly fine. Whatever book Tessa had probably seen me reading was just a novel I was recategorizing. I'd had to open it to check the copyright page or something. *Nothing to see here, girls. Nothing at all.*

"We could go now," I suggested. "Let me double-check with Aunt Laura."

"Is the shop open?" Tessa was still looking at me like I'd morphed into a cat, but I ignored her.

"Should be," Izzy said.

Amelia was on her feet faster than I thought she could get there after being all sunk down in the beanbag chair, her hair as wild as usual. Izzy held her hands out for Tessa and Amelia to help her up, even though I was closer to her. They pulled her out of the chair more for fun than because she needed the help.

I spotted Amelia's phone lying on the floor and scooped it up for her.

"Oh!" She held her hand over her mouth. "Thank you!"

"That would make this . . . oh, the twenty-third time," I joked.

"In a week," Izzy added.

Amelia looped her purse over her arm and dropped her phone inside. She patted the bright-red leather. "There. Safe."

"Until we get to the ice cream parlor," I said.

My friend laughed. "O ye of little faith."

"That's correct. I have little faith you're not going to lose that thing."

Which reminded me of her losing it at the barn, so I quickly dove into the story of meeting that cranky old guy who asked me to stay on.

"That's great," Izzy said, with a little bit of the familiar Izzy enthusiasm coming back. Animals would generally cause that in her.

She was right. It *was* great, and I reminded myself to focus on that rather than on what I was going to lose. I hated that I tended to camp on the negative things rather than look to the positive.

After getting the okay from Aunt Laura, we walked to the ice cream shop, our good-natured bantering and laughter surrounding us. The heat was stifling, and by the time we walked into the air-conditioned shop, our conversation centered around which flavors of ice cream we wanted. Amelia was practically drooling over the flavor descriptions on the wall.

"*Cookie dough crumble,*" she read. "*Mega chunks of dough with caramel streams swirling around creamy vanilla ice cream, loaded with nuggets of decadent dark chocolate.*"

Okay, so my own mouth was watering too.

"What about that one?" Izzy pointed toward a pan in the display case containing something that looked like M&Ms mixed into blue ice cream.

While the other girls debated the merits of French vanilla versus vanilla bean, I was silently trying to figure out how to make sure the conversation stayed away from me and on them. I never was one to talk a lot about myself, though these friends had slowly tried to pull me out of my shell. I appreciated it most days.

"Your turn, Shay." Amelia poked me.

I still hadn't made up my mind.

"Just *pick* one," Amelia said in mock frustration and caught a drip trickling down her cone.

Izzy pushed her way to the display case. "She'll have the peppermint marshmallow cream—two scoops. Waffle cone."

I grinned. Sure. Why not?

Tessa had staked out a table in the corner of the shop so we could enjoy the air conditioning as long as possible.

"Are you happy you're finished with *Annie*?" I asked Amelia. Her entire world had revolved around the production for six weeks, and I still hadn't sat down and talked with her one-on-one about it. Ugh. I hated that I didn't know how to be a good friend. I was learning. But still . . .

Amelia took my question and ran with it, and between her and Izzy, who shared at least 75 percent of Amelia's theater enthusiasm, they managed to fill a lot of talk time. Tessa and I sat back and enjoyed our ice cream and asked questions. I didn't mind. Tessa didn't either. We'd get our chance eventually. After twenty minutes of theater-centric talk, Tessa turned to me as I popped the last of my cone into my mouth.

"Are you working much for your aunt this summer?"

"Some," I said, covering my mouth. "But not as much as I used to."

"How often do you have to work on alphabetizing?"

I hesitated. She was getting close to home here, and I couldn't let that happen.

Luckily, Izzy saved me without realizing it. She got a notification on her phone and started to squeal. "Look, look!"

She turned the phone toward Tessa and me, and we watched a TikTok video of a dog dancing on its hind legs, wearing a tutu.

Saved by the dog.

"I need to get back to the store to finish up," I said, standing. "But you guys feel free to stay and enjoy more ice cream." I laughed, but I didn't feel anything close to the joy I wanted to feel.

None of them seemed to notice my evasion. At least that's what I thought until I saw Tessa's eyes. I saw concern in them, and I had a feeling that if I stayed any longer, she was going to ask me if I was okay.

It would have been a lie to say I was.

Sure enough, a few minutes after I got back to the store, my phone buzzed with a text from Tessa.

Tessa: What's going on? Are you okay?

I didn't want to blow her off. She cared about me. I also knew I couldn't tell her the truth.

Me: I'm okay! ☺

Tessa: You don't seem like yourself.

Maybe if I redirected, she'd let it go.

Me: Hard stuff in that journal.

Tessa: Yes. There totally was.

Me: Gotta process through it all, you know?

Tessa: Pray?

I stared at my screen. She was right. Had I prayed about *any* of this? Maybe that was one thing I could open up about.

Me: I don't even know what to pray.

Almost a minute passed before Tessa's response popped up. It doesn't have to be anything fancy. Just cry out. Like David.

In my heart, I knew she was right. David faced a lot of bad

stuff in his day, more than I ever would, but he was also a king appointed by God. That kind of made it hard to relate to him. Did God truly care about little Shay Mitchell? Didn't He have more important things to deal with?

Me: I'm trying to trust.

Tessa: I think that's all God wants from us.

Me: My mom was a Christian, so it's hard to make sense of what she did.

Tessa: I know. I get it.

Of course she did. And wasn't Tessa's dad a Christian too? I sent her a palm-to-forehead emoji. The next message I sent read: How could she think it was right?

Tessa: I guess we won't ever know what she was thinking. Unless you found something else in the journal?

I *had* read in the journal that Mom didn't want to have kids—which meant me. And what if I'd disappointed her even after I was born? Maybe she would have preferred a boy, or for me to cry less, or . . .

Tessa: You're loved, Shay. No matter what your mom said about being pregnant. Remember, she wrote that before she met you.

Me: Thank you.

I meant it. Her words helped ease a little of my pain.

But not my guilt.

Chapter
23

On Thursday afternoon when Aunt Laura dropped me off at Green Tree—um, Second Chance Farm—I felt numb. The entire farm looked different. The horses hanging their heads over their stall doors weren't the familiar ones I'd come to love. These were strange, new animals.

The first horse I came to was a chestnut gelding with a wide blaze on his face and a pink nose. He was almost pony sized but had the muscles of a quarter horse, which is what I guessed he was.

I went over to him, and he immediately stuck his nose on my cheek and sniffed my hair. It made me laugh without thinking.

"What are you doing, boy?"

I could feel his breath on my neck, and I reached up to pet him.

"That's Blaze."

Link came up behind me.

"He's cute," I said.

"Acts more like a dog than a horse."

Blaze started rubbing his head against my arm to scratch himself, and it threw me off balance.

"So, why are you here?"

I turned to the old man. He wore a red ball cap with a sweat stain along the brim and what looked like the same short-sleeved plaid shirt he'd been wearing when I met him.

"Didn't you want me to come?" I hoped I hadn't misheard him.

"Yep, but that wasn't the question."

"Uh . . . I don't understand."

Blaze went back to his hay net, but I almost thought he was still eyeing me as if he, too, was waiting to find out why the strange girl was here.

"For the horses?" I finally said.

Link chuckled. "Darn horse girls."

I was pretty sure he didn't mean it to sound unkind, but it reminded me of Janie's rant.

"Denise is my daughter, by the way," Link said. "She and Brad are the ones who wanted to expand the ministry, and I went along for the ride. No pun intended."

"What exactly do you guys do?"

I walked over to the next stall, where a stocky black horse with a smaller white blaze on his face stared out at me. He didn't hang his head over the stall, and he wasn't eating his hay. He seemed to be watching me, his ears pricked forward.

"We try to touch people's lives with horses." Link crossed his arms and leaned against the side of Blaze's stall. "Sometimes it's in big ways, other times small. But horses will touch us one way or another."

"Yeah," I said. The black horse took a step toward me, extending his nose. He didn't seem scared or even all that curious, but he came over anyway, and I realized how large he was. I was used to dainty Ava, but even though this horse wasn't incredibly tall, he was bulky, with a wide barrel.

"We call him Tank," Link said.

I smiled. That fit him.

I went down the line and met the others. There were ten of them in all. Most of them were quarter horses, but an off-the-track thoroughbred and a Welsh pony rounded out the mix.

When I got to the last stall, I did a double take. The paint mare Sky stared back at me.

"Why's she still here?"

Link came over too. "Came with the farm."

"What?"

"Owner surrender. Didn't pay their bills or something."

"So she's staying?" I said.

"You ask a lot of questions." Link handed me a broom. "Sweep. And yes, she's staying."

I took the broom. How could her owners have left her? I didn't think I would ever fully understand how some people treated horses. Or even how some people treated people. I thought again of my mom and started sweeping faster.

"Dad teaching you the ropes?"

Denise walked into the barn as I was finishing the aisle. I made sure to get every last piece of hay and dirt. I wanted to make a good impression, or else they might regret their decision to have me here.

I nodded.

"How old are you, Shay?"

"Almost sixteen."

"What's your story with horses?"

Speaking of asking a lot of questions . . .

I tried to read Denise's face. She seemed open and real, like she was asking me because she really wanted to know the answer, not because she thought she had to make small talk. "I've always loved horses," I said. "When I was a little girl, my dad let me believe that someday I would have my own."

Denise smiled. "Did you?"

"Oh, I wish."

"Have you ridden at all?"

"Took a few lessons last year, and I watch all the videos I can on YouTube."

"That's great. Who's your favorite trainer?"

Last year, I would've said Mason King, but after that clinic, I'd stopped watching his videos for a while. I'd started watching them again a few weeks ago, analyzing much more than the training methods. At the clinic, I thought I'd seen the real man behind the persona he'd created. But outside of horses, outside of the pizzazz of the spotlight, who was my father, really?

"I used to like Mason King," I said.

Denise was nodding. She went over to Sky's stall and watched the mare eating hay for a minute. I joined her, sort of hoping she'd tell me her opinion of Mason.

"Let's take her to the round pen," she said.

"You have a round pen?"

That's when I saw the rope halter hanging from her arm. She handed it to me. I tied it to Sky and led her from the stall.

"Yep, set it up yesterday."

A rush of excitement hit me. Janie preferred working with horses in the big arena, as did her boarders, so she'd never had a round pen. It wasn't that you couldn't effectively work with horses in arenas, but I'd seen so many videos where trainers utilized round pens. Mason King had one at his clinic.

"She's a pretty mare," Denise said.

"How could someone leave her?" I asked, patting Sky's neck.

"We all do stupid stuff sometimes."

"Yeah," I agreed. *Don't I know it.*

Chapter
24

THE ROUND PEN WAS LITERALLY THAT—a round pen made up of twelve metal-rung fence panels and one gate that created a circle so horses couldn't hide in a corner. I led Sky into the pen while Denise stayed outside to instruct me on what to do. For a second, my heart raced. I'd dreamed of working with horses in this way, but I'd never had the chance.

The July sun shone down on us, and all I could think was how much I wished my dad, the one who raised me, were here to see this. Oh, I hoped he would be proud of me.

"Go ahead and take her halter off," Denise said. Her wide-brimmed cowboy hat and sunglasses made it hard for me to read her expressions. She rested her arms on one of the rails, her foot on a lower rung, like she watched inexperienced teen girls pretend they knew what they were doing with horses every day.

I did what she said and held on to the halter and the lead,

intending to use the rope to drive the horse around the pen like I'd seen other trainers do.

My phone buzzed in my pocket, and I wondered what Izzy would think of this right now. She would probably want to be in the round pen too. I pulled out my phone to take a quick picture to text to her.

"See what she did there?" Denise called.

I glanced up. Sky had taken a few steps away from me.

"When you got distracted, she felt that."

I sheepishly re-pocketed my phone. "Sorry."

"There's no judgment here, Shay." Denise's tone was warm. "Just observing. We're not meant to be burdened with devices every second of the day."

It was the same thing Grams had been trying to tell me in the coffee shop, but the way Denise said it was so much easier to accept. I twirled the lead rope like I'd practiced so many times by myself with no horse.

Sky's head lifted.

"What do you want me to do here?" I asked.

"Whatever seems right to you."

I wondered how Mason King would approach the situation. Round pens were used for lots of training exercises, but often it was about gaining the horse's respect. Whoever was able to get the horse to move its feet was the boss. It mimicked a herd environment, where the lead horse moves the others around.

I made a clicking sound with my mouth and twirled the rope toward Sky's rear.

She just stood there.

Okay, try again. I backed up a few steps, clicked, and swung the end of the lead rope at her side. I didn't touch her with the rope, but it came close. She flicked an ear at me and cocked her back leg, completely ignoring me. That was not the response I saw in videos.

I gathered the rope in my left hand and kept clicking. "Come on, Sky. Move."

She glanced at me, then took a few very slow steps.

I clicked again, and she walked a bit more.

"Go, girl!"

Sky turned to face me. I moved toward her hind end, swinging the lead rope more. The horse moved her butt out of the way but kept turning in to me every time I moved. I wanted her to move out and around the pen. Why wasn't she?

I spun the rope as fast as I could and let the end smack into her side. That got her attention. She sidestepped away from me, making a small grunting sound like I'd hurt her, and I immediately flashed back to the clinic where my bio father had whipped Ava when she didn't do what he wanted. Oh, gosh, I didn't want to be like that. Not now, not ever.

I eyed Denise and hoped I didn't look too stupid. She hadn't said anything, but I wasn't sure if that was good or bad. Nothing like an audience for your first time trying something you didn't have a clue how to do.

Go, mare. Move.

I pictured myself in an arena with the audience watching me work a troubled horse no one could tame. I was focused, determined, and the horse would make a complete turnaround. People would call me a gifted horse whisperer!

Except Sky was barely listening to me.

"What am I doing wrong?" I said, slapping the end of the lead rope onto the ground near Sky. She took a few steps, then stopped.

"What are you trying to get her to do?" Denise responded.

"Uh . . . move?"

"Okay, but what it looks like from here is that you don't know what you are asking her to do. You want her to move, but how? Walk? Trot? Which direction?"

"I don't really care."

Denise grinned. "Exactly. She can't know what you want if you don't even know what that is. Decide what you want, and then ask her to do it. She still has a choice, but horses want us to be clear with what we ask. No wishy-washy requests for them."

I guess that made sense.

"I want you to make up your mind very clearly regarding what you want from Sky right here."

Whew. Okay. I needed to do this.

"Use the rope to drive her away from you, but really focus your energy."

"I don't want to be mean," I said.

Denise pointed at the mare. "You can be firm while still being kind."

I didn't want to tell her about my experience with Mason King, but I needed to explain some of why I was hesitating. "Sky's owner abandoned her, and she's been through a lot. It feels wrong to drive her away."

"Why?" Denise asked.

It was a good question I needed to answer, but I wasn't sure why I was suddenly hesitating. Was it because I'd been abandoned too, so I related to the mare?

"Shay, one thing horses need most is security. They need to know they are safe. They often look to the herd leader to give them that, and if there's no leader, they become anxious. You can help Sky the most by showing you will be that leader for her in a fair way."

"By making her move?"

"In this case, yes. There is a direct correlation here to life. If we just let stuff happen to us without any goals or dreams, then we're going to float along and be moved by everything that hits us, rather than specifically working toward things."

I tried to concentrate and listen to this woman. I wasn't convinced working a horse in a round pen was going to have an impact on my real life. Could it make Izzy talk to me like she used to? Or change the fact that I couldn't begin to understand why my parents—biological and adopted—had acted the ways they had? Could anything change how I'd been reading dirty books and was pushing God further and further away from my life?

I pointed to my right, where I wanted Sky to go, and clicked with my mouth.

The mare ignored me, so I swung the rope.

"Use that rope smoothly, and gradually increase the pressure if needed. If she doesn't listen, you can touch her with it."

Okay, girl. We can do this.

I increased the speed of my swinging, and that seemed to at least get Sky's attention. She looked at me. I let the end of the rope tap her side.

Focus. What do I want?

"This is for your own good!" I said. "Trust me."

Sky eventually perked up enough to walk off, away from my rope.

"There. Release your pressure now since she did what you asked," Denise said.

I did, praising Sky. "Good girl."

"Ask again, and this time expect her to respond quicker."

We repeated the process three times, and then Denise asked me to increase my pressure again until Sky was trotting. The mare listened much quicker, and in a few minutes, I had her continually trotting around the pen.

"She's paying attention now," Denise said with a smile. "Notice how her ear is turned toward you."

I couldn't help the huge grin I felt spread across my face. Oh my word. I was actually doing it! Working with a horse in a round pen!

"When you're ready, slow your body down, let out a breath, and ask her to stop."

I exhaled and said "Whoa," and that's all it took. Sky put on the brakes and immediately stopped, turning in to me.

"Good job," Denise said.

I laughed. "That's so cool."

"You do know a thing or two about horses, Shay."

I walked over to the mare and touched her on the forehead, then scratched her neck. She sighed. Denise came into the pen and petted Sky too.

"This is the type of stuff we do with our horses here," Denise said, tipping her hat up a little. "We help people make sense of life while working with a horse. Horses are great teachers."

I let out a smirk before I could help myself. "I sure need to make sense of my life."

"We all do at some point or another . . . and often multiple times in our lives. When someone lets us down, horse or human, it's easy to allow that disappointment to dictate our whole world." She took off her sunglasses and placed them on top of her hat. "Hurt does things like that. But when we've felt abandoned, it's important to remember that we are never truly alone."

"Sometimes it feels like it," I said.

"Yes, it does," Denise said. "But God will never leave us. Even if everyone else does."

I gave Sky some more scratches. Her skin was warm. I'd probably need to hose her off. Her pink nostrils flared a little. She probably hadn't been worked in a long time.

"What you said about Sky is true," Denise said. "She was abandoned. That's a terrible thing that shouldn't have happened to her. But think about it from this new perspective: She gets to stay here and meet new people who will love her the way she's meant to be loved. That wouldn't have happened if her old owners had kept her."

"Are you saying bad things happen for a reason?" I didn't love that concept now any more than I had when my friends had talked about it.

Denise reached out and patted Sky's rump. "I'm saying God can use the broken things in our lives for good even when they suck. We can learn and grow from everything that happens."

A truck pulled up near the barn, and Denise glanced at her watch.

"That's my vet. Wasn't supposed to be here for another half hour."

"I better go, then."

"Stay with Sky as long as you want. Just put her in her stall when you're done."

Denise left us in the round pen, and I stood there staring at the horse, trying to decide if what the woman had told me made sense. I pulled out my phone and found a text.

Izzy: What's up?

It was only a line, but I took it as a win. I walked to the round pen gate, and when I turned around, there was Sky, right behind me.

Chapter
25

A HALF HOUR LATER, I texted my aunt to pick me up and waited for her while sitting outside the barn, sweaty but happy. I was still thinking about my experience in the round pen. I wasn't sure what to make of it in some ways, but what if Denise was right about God using broken things?

I decided to text Izzy as if everything were okay between us.

Me: At the barn. Cool experience with horse in round pen.

Oh?! she texted back immediately. What happened?

Me: That Denise lady had me work with Sky.

Izzy: Which one is that?

Sometimes I forgot that my friends couldn't always remember the names of the horses. I typed back: The paint mare.

Izzy: Did I meet her?

Me: Yep.

Izzy: Did you get to ride?

Me: Nope. Stayed on ground.

Something else non-horse people didn't always understand was that much of the work with horses happened before you ever sat in the saddle. Riding was not like it was often portrayed in the movies. You didn't just get on a horse and gallop off into the sunset, as much as I wished that were true.

"Hey there, kid."

I looked up to see Link standing behind me. He took a swig from a water bottle and tossed me one too. I barely caught it.

"Thanks," I said.

"Good work out there."

I unscrewed the lid of the bottle. He'd been watching me?

"Thanks," I said. "Are you going to keep Sky?"

He gave a shrug. "That's up to Denise."

"I hope you do."

Link chuckled. "Something tells me you'd want to keep every horse you ever met."

He wasn't entirely wrong.

My phone buzzed.

Izzy: Can I come ride sometime?

I almost texted her back an immediate no, but I felt relieved she still wanted to do things with me. Maybe our relationship wasn't as fractured as it had felt a few days ago.

"I am a little crazy in the horse department," I said.

Link took another gulp from his water. "Ah, my Denise is too."

I didn't mind being compared to her. She had a steadiness about her that the horses seemed to like, and I did too.

"Horses don't seem to care if we have strong feelings," I said.

"Nope." He leaned against the barn doorframe, removing his cap and wiping his sweaty forehead with his arm. "As long as we're fair about things. Doesn't make sense, does it? An animal that'll spook at a five-pound rabbit doesn't mind our thousand-pound feelings."

I wished people could be more like horses. Apparently, horses could handle more than humans in a lot of ways.

"You got a ride home?" Link finished his water, crumpled the bottle, and screwed the lid back on it.

"My aunt." I checked my phone. It had been ten minutes since I'd texted her. She usually texted right back. I sent another.

Me: I'm ready. ETA?

"Live nearby?" Link asked.

"In town. My aunt owns a bookstore."

"Booked Up?"

"Yep."

He nodded. "Nice store."

I didn't know why, but Link hadn't struck me as the reading type. One more aspect about me that I wasn't thrilled about—unfair assumptions. Probably one of the many reasons I was considering giving Mason King another chance.

My phone vibrated, but it was Amelia on our group thread, not Aunt Laura.

Amelia: We should do ice cream again! Soon!

Me: It was delicious!!!

Ten minutes later, after my friends and I had texted about future ice cream flavors we wanted to try, my aunt still hadn't gotten back to me. Sometimes she left her phone in the storeroom or bookstore office, but she usually kept it with her on the days I was working to avoid situations like this. I tried calling the bookstore.

"Booked Up, how can I help you?" the girl on the other end said. It was Ginny, an employee who'd been working there for a few years.

"Hey, is Aunt Laura around?"

"Thought she was with you."

"Uh, no."

"She left a half hour ago to get you."

I thanked her and hung up, then sent my aunt another text.

Me: **Where are you???**

Traffic could sometimes get a little dicey in town. Maybe there was a construction detour that I missed on our way over.

Another ten minutes passed, and I tried to distract myself with YouTube videos. The latest Mason King video featured him working with a horse in a round pen. Obviously, it would be an entirely different event than what I'd just experienced, so I decided not to watch it right then. Maybe later. Maybe never.

A familiar SUV pulled up in the small lot, and I stood up, instantly on edge.

Grams rushed out of the car and over to me. She was supposed to be at the cottage. If she was here instead, then something was definitely wrong.

"Where's Aunt Laura?" I asked.

My grandmother, the poised older woman with never a white hair out of place, looked frazzled. "I'll explain everything in the car. Let's go."

Oh no. Please no.

"Is she okay? What's going on?"

Grams paused, and that was all it took for fear to grab hold of me like the monster it was, squeezing my head as if to crush it. I could feel the presence of someone behind me. Out of the corner of my eye, I saw it was Denise. She didn't say anything, but I figured she was probably wondering what was going on too.

My grandmother inhaled and looked me straight in the eyes. "Your aunt was in an accident."

Chapter
26

I'D HAD THREE MOMENTS in my life when time felt like it didn't exist, when I was suspended between real life and something else, something darker, that threatened to eat me alive in every way but the literal sense.

The first time was when I'd woken up in the hospital after the car wreck with my dad and found out he didn't make it. Nothing can prepare someone for a moment like that. You might think you'll be strong and take the news with grace and dignity, but in the end, we're all hardwired to receive bad news the same way— a punch to the gut that knocks the wind out of us.

The second was the day my aunt told me who my bio father was. At least Mason King was still alive, but it also hit me hard, finding out my father was the man I'd been following on YouTube for years. The third was when Grams dropped the bomb that my mother had left me.

Today was a different kind of shock.

It was like all the feelings of those other events combined, and I felt them trample me like a stampede of horses driven mad with their need to escape. I felt mangled, and each second that passed was another kick to my chest.

I had never understood why people passed out when receiving bad news, but as my grandmother went out of focus, my legs buckled and I stumbled. I didn't fall, because several strong hands grabbed on to me and held me up. Denise on my right, Link on my left, and Grams right in front of me.

"Shay, she's okay," Grams said. "She's okay. But we need to get to the hospital."

I was hyperventilating, I think. I was breathing in and out, but it didn't feel like any of the oxygen was reaching me.

"I . . . I . . . what . . ."

"Get in and we'll go."

I finally managed to move my legs and climb into her vehicle. Grams had to help me with my seat belt like I was new to the concept.

"She's going to die," I whispered, and then said it again, rocking a little as we drove toward the road, muttering the words like a mantra I couldn't control.

"Calm down."

"I can't lose someone else. I can't!"

Grams's voice got louder. "She is not dying."

"Everyone always leaves me!"

"Shay, she is *not* dying."

I swung toward her. "What's *wrong* with me?"

Grams slammed on the brakes at the end of the driveway. "Shay, stop it!"

I felt like she'd slapped me. But maybe her tone was what I needed to jar me out of the hole of fear and panic I'd fallen into. We sat silent for a moment, her turn signal clicking, my heart pounding. The air conditioning struggled to keep up with the heat. When the car started moving again, I took a breath and let it out. "What happened?" I asked.

"I don't know for sure, but they brought her in to check her out thoroughly."

I closed my eyes and desperately attempted to convince myself to believe my grandmother. "Are you sure?" I asked.

"She called me herself."

I covered my mouth. "She did?"

"Yes. It's okay."

"How can you know?"

"Because I talked to her."

"What happened?" I asked again.

Grams glanced over at me. "I don't know. She wasn't able to stay on the line."

"Because she was hurt?"

"No. Because a nurse had just come to check her vitals."

"Please hurry."

"I'm doing my best, Shay," Grams said, obviously holding back growing irritation.

By the time we got to the hospital, I had calmed down a little. I felt wobbly but was able to follow Grams into the building. I trailed behind as she grilled the nurses on where we could find my aunt and convinced them we were indeed her family, even if technically Grams was not. We found Aunt Laura in a curtained partition in the ER.

She didn't look as bad as I had feared, but there was a bruise on her forehead, and she winced when she repositioned herself in the bed. She was wearing her normal clothes, so I guessed it was a good sign that they hadn't cut anything off.

"Hey, kiddo." Aunt Laura waved me over.

I hesitated. I could smell a combination of antiseptic and unidentifiable scents, and everything in me wanted to escape this building in which people both healed and died.

"Sorry I didn't text you back," my aunt said, giving me a feeble grin.

I nodded, still mute, and then went to her.

Aunt Laura grabbed my hand. Her fingers were cold.

"I didn't want to scare you," she said. "But I'm sure I did."

"Are you okay?"

"Yeah, kid." My aunt smiled, but I could see the pain in her eyes.

"Are you hurt?"

"Well, I now know airbags work, let me tell you." She chuckled. "Some whiplash, a headache. I'll be fine."

I squeezed her hand harder than I meant to. "Are you sure?"

"Only reason I'm still in the ER is that so many people decided to have emergencies at the same time." My aunt looked toward Grams. "Thanks for bringing her, but she should go home. I'll have Ginny or someone pick me up later."

"I'm not going anywhere," I said.

She gave my hand a little squeeze. "I don't want—or need—you to stay. I only wanted you to come to see that I'm okay. What I need is for you to go home, walk Stanley, and take care of the store."

"I can't."

"Yes, you can." Aunt Laura patted my arm with her other hand. "I'll be home in no time."

I so appreciated that Aunt Laura wanted to spare me the experience of sitting in a hospital and all the memories that would dredge up, but she didn't have any other immediate family to be there for her. I didn't want her to be alone.

"Please." My aunt gave my hand another squeeze, then let go. "Do that for me, all right?"

I forced myself to stand a little taller and be a big girl. I would do that for my aunt. I could fall apart later, if I had to, but right now she needed to know I could handle this.

"Promise you won't be late for dinner," I tried to joke, "because I'm not reheating it for you."

My aunt chuckled, then winced again. "Oh, gosh, Shay, don't make me laugh."

As we walked out of the hospital, I ripped out my phone and texted the girls.

Me: Aunt Laura in car accident.

Within a minute, my phone blew up.

Amelia: OMG WHAT?????? IS SHE OK??

Izzy: Oh no, what happened?

Tessa: Praying right now!

Amelia: Please let us know!

Izzy: Where is she?

I texted back: ER. Will be ok.

Tessa: Are you home?

Me: Heading there.

Tessa: I'm babysitting Logan or I'd be there.

Izzy: Same! Watching Sebastian.

Amelia: I'm babysitting for my parents. They're at counseling. I can come over after if they let me take the car.

Me: It's ok. I'll be ok.

Tessa: Lord Jesus, we pray for Laura and ask You to be with her and Shay right now.

"Shay, get off your phone."

I looked up at Grams. She was several feet in front of me in the parking lot, and I had nearly walked into a van while I was texting.

Me: I'll keep ya posted.

Chapter
27

"ARE YOU POSITIVE YOU'RE GOING TO BE ALL RIGHT?"

My grandmother asked the question, but she was already scooting toward the apartment door. Stanley leaned against my leg, giving more comfort than Grams was. She'd kept herself together in the hospital, but she'd been uncharacteristically fidgety on the way home. I had a feeling the experience had brought up a lot of memories for her, too. How could it not?

"I'm fine," I said.

I cringed at my lie. Hadn't I adamantly told my aunt only a few short days ago that I didn't lie? It used to be true. Dad taught me that the truth was more important than getting away with anything. But lately . . .

Grams paused, giving me a good once-over, like she was that defense lawyer I'd imagined before, trying to tell if her client was giving her the runaround.

"You have my number," she said. Then, without warning, she

came over and gave me a sideways hug. Hugging my bony grand-mother was like hugging a fence post. This time, her hug was so fast I didn't have time to return it.

And then she was gone. Stanley stared at me down his long nose, his pleading eyes begging for his dinner. He had no idea of the turmoil his humans were experiencing, and I didn't know whether he would've cared as long as he got fed.

Feeding him and Matilda distracted me for a few minutes, but after that I couldn't stop worrying about Aunt Laura. I checked my phone, but she hadn't contacted me. Would they keep her this long if she was okay? Of course, emergency departments were often backlogged, but if she was okay, why hadn't they discharged her?

I texted my friends: I'm home.

None of them got back to me. I decided to go down into the store to check on things like my aunt had asked me to do. I found Ginny at the checkout counter.

The twenty-something woman with tattoos down her arms saw me, and her eyes went wide. "Oh, gosh, is she okay?"

"Yeah," I said, half expecting Ginny to hug me too. She gave off a tough-girl vibe but wasn't nearly as tough inside as she made people think.

"Have you heard from her?" I asked.

Ginny shook her head.

"I thought she might ask you for a ride."

"Radio silence here," Ginny said.

"Same." I held up my phone.

Ginny asked me what happened, and I told her the little I knew.

"Wow, she's lucky."

I agreed, though Tessa would've said it was God protecting my aunt. Was that true? I didn't know.

I offered to help in the store, but Ginny waved me off.

"We're good here. Go get some rest."

I didn't tell her I would probably be doing anything but resting considering how wired I felt, but I appreciated that I wouldn't have to smile and pretend everything was fine in front of customers. I climbed back up the stairs to the apartment. Stanley greeted me like I'd been gone the whole day.

A text came in, and I yanked my phone from my pocket.

Aunt Laura: They want to keep me overnight.

Me: WHAT??

Aunt Laura: It's only a precaution. I'm okay.

Me: Then why are they keeping you??

Aunt Laura: Concussion, some brain swelling on CT scan.

Me: Oh no!

Aunt Laura: Not too serious. Don't worry, okay?

Me: Too late!

Aunt Laura: LOL. They think I'll be fine. I should be home tomorrow. I promise.

How could she promise that? She'd thought she was coming home this afternoon! I wanted to throw my phone across the room. No. This was completely unfair.

Me: Can I come stay with you?

Aunt Laura: No, I want you there.

Me: I can ask Ginny to bring me.

Aunt Laura: Emphatic no, kiddo. Stanley and Matilda need you.

I wanted to type back *But I need YOU*, except I didn't want her to worry any more than she already was.

Aunt Laura: Ask your grandmother to come stay with you.

Me: She didn't go back to the cottage?

Aunt Laura: Not until I come home. She'll want to help.

Me: Um, no thanks.

Aunt Laura: LOL. I figured. I'll have my phone. You can text me, but they gave me some pain meds so might end up falling asleep.

Me: OK.

Aunt Laura: Don't worry.

Fat chance. Ugh.

Aunt Laura: I'm really sorry.

Me: Not your fault!

Aunt Laura: We'll get through this, Shay. I'm not going anywhere.

Me: OK.

Aunt Laura: I love you.

I froze at that last text. I don't think my aunt had ever said those words directly to me before, even though it was obvious she cared about me. I stared at my phone screen as it went blurry from my tears.

Me: Love you too.

Chapter

28

I TRIED TO KEEP MY NIGHTTIME ROUTINE NORMAL, but how could anything be normal when Aunt Laura lay in some hospital bed, eating disgusting hospital food, probably unable to sleep because of all the beeping and talking and noise? And I was here, stuck in the silence, unable to do a thing to help her.

I'd texted the girls an update, and they all were sympathetic, offering to pray and stay in touch. They meant it. They really did. But my brain was going a mile a minute, like a bolting horse, and I couldn't seem to slow it down. I tried turning on the TV and blasting one of Izzy's favorite *Cupcake Wars* episodes to have some background noise, but that only stressed me out more because I wished she were here with me, spouting nonstop commentary on what was happening in the show.

What I wanted was to not be alone, but my friends hadn't been able to come over, and I couldn't bring myself to ask them.

"Guess it's just you and me," I said to Stanley. He was so dead to the world in sleep, like any self-respecting greyhound should be at ten o'clock at night, that he didn't even flinch. I should be asleep too.

I brushed my teeth and got dressed for bed, but I couldn't bring myself to climb under my covers. Instead, I lay down on the sofa, pulled my knees toward my chest, and worried about my aunt. She was the only blood family I had left. My adoptive grandparents still counted for something, but it was hard to feel affection for them like they wanted me to.

I scrolled through the contacts on my phone, searching for someone who might be up to chat with me, but I didn't have many people who fit that category. Izzy, Tessa, and Amelia were in my favorites section, as were Aunt Laura and Janie, though I didn't know if I'd ever see that woman again. Everyone else was either a casual acquaintance from school or someone I didn't trust quite enough for a moment like this.

I sent another group text to the girls.

Me: Anyone up?

I waited.

And waited.

My screen went black twice, and I woke it up each time, hoping for that lifeline of a vibration in my hand that showed someone cared.

What if my aunt died?

The thought hit me square in the gut.

It had already crossed my mind when I saw my grandmother at the barn and she wouldn't tell me what was wrong. I'd immediately imagined the worst-case scenario, fighting my thoughts every step of the way to not go down that dark road. But I could not lose someone else. God wouldn't allow that, right? He couldn't. I wouldn't be able to bear it, and didn't He say He wouldn't let us be tempted beyond what we could bear? And if He's not going to tempt us beyond what we can bear, shouldn't He also limit the heartbreak we have to endure?

Yet God allowed Mom to leave and Dad to die.

What kind of a God *did* that? I mean, really. I didn't think even Zoe would have an answer for that. I silently fumed as I found the Zs in my contacts. I was going to ask her. I tapped out a text and hit send before I could backtrack.

Me: I don't understand why God allows suffering.

There. See what she thought of *that*. I wasn't sure even a youth leader could give me a good answer.

My friends still hadn't gotten back to me. Could they all be asleep? Why hadn't Amelia come over like she said she would? Her parents' counseling probably went longer than expected.

I got up and started pacing the small apartment. My insides churned like a washing machine, with so many questions and doubts that it scared me. Where was the faith I'd had as a kid? I could remember being only five or six years old and holding my daddy's hand as we walked into church. I was excited to meet God behind those pretty doors, learn about His love, and hear about people who'd been heroes . . . like David facing Goliath, Esther saving her people, Noah building the ark, Jesus feeding five thousand. Those stories had come to life for me, and in my childlike mind they were as real as my dad.

As I'd told Izzy, it wasn't that I didn't believe in God anymore. I could never fully turn my back on Him. But there was a whole lot of gray space between being devoted and completely rejecting Him. I thought about all the times I'd supported my friends in spiritual things. I'd shared Scriptures, I'd prayed, I'd gone to youth group with them. That wasn't an act, was it? I really believed those things, didn't I?

I paced to the kitchen table and dropped my phone on the wooden surface. Yeah, I believed. At least I thought I did. Being real was important to me, so I wouldn't have made stuff like that up.

Back to the sofa.

I ran my fingers through my hair. When was the last time I had washed it? I probably still smelled like the barn.

Back to the table.

Was I a fraud? Telling the truth *did* matter to me. If I truly believed the Bible and what I'd been taught growing up, it made sense I'd share it with my friends.

My feet took me to the sofa again.

Then what about the doubts? Denise had said God would never leave me. Did that mean He was here with me right now in this hollow apartment that screamed of my aunt's absence?

All the questions squeezed my mind, and I couldn't handle another one. I went to my bedroom, slipped the erotic novel out from under my bed, and took it into the living room. There was no risk that my aunt or my friends would see. I had free rein. Absolutely no one could call me out on anything tonight. And I desperately needed the distraction from my pounding thoughts and questions.

I read several chapters and shoved away every wave of guilt that tried to surface. I skimmed words until I got to the scenes describing the acts I knew full well only husbands and wives should share. But right then, I didn't care. If God was going to allow my family to fall apart and be destroyed like He had, then why should I respect His rules?

I kept reading even though I knew I shouldn't. Besides, I rationalized, I didn't understand half of what I read. At one point, I reached for my phone and typed a question into Google. I scrolled through the results, and the descriptions of the articles were almost as graphic as the novel. But while the book was fiction, and I didn't know how much was based on reality, these informational pieces were real life.

My pulse was pounding now, and I was feeling stuff in my body I had never felt before. That should have clued me in on how much I was being affected by the words, but I didn't want to stop. I wasn't thinking about my aunt or my parents or even the horses from Green Tree Farm I'd bonded with and would probably never see again. Those negative thoughts were finally silenced because I was so engrossed in the words I read.

But I didn't stop there.

I should have stopped. I could practically feel my dad's presence hovering over me, trying to keep me from being so stupid. But in that moment, I wanted to scream at him, *You left me!!!!!* My parents had no right to influence me after their deaths. They weren't here. They didn't know the *me* I was right now.

One of the articles on Google had pictures. They were only drawings, but they were graphic and illustrated what I'd read. I stared at them for far longer than I intended. Without thinking it through, I backed up to my search and clicked on *Images*.

What I saw shocked me, and I instinctively wanted to look away. Good girls—*especially girls*, I thought—didn't look at stuff like this.

And yet I did.

When I set my phone down an hour later, I saw I had missed multiple text messages from Tessa. I blushed. I couldn't read any of them right then. The shame I felt from giving in to my curiosity was almost as overwhelming as the emotions that caused me to start reading in the first place.

I covered my face with both hands, trying to make sense of what I'd done. Accidentally seeing a pornographic photo because you typed something weird into a search engine was one thing. But I had purposely gone looking for them. Shame threatened to drown me.

I finally opened my texts.

Tessa: How are you holding up?

With a shaking hand, I texted my friend back.

Me: Not great.

And *that*, I could emphatically say, was the truth.

Chapter
29

Tessa offered to take me to the farm in the morning. That's what her other texts had been about last night. I had reluctantly accepted her ride because I would go crazy if I had to stay in the apartment by myself for an entire day thinking about Aunt Laura. Working in the bookstore would be even worse as I rounded every corner, expecting to run into her.

Tessa knew me well enough to understand that the best way to get me out of a funk was to involve animals.

I climbed into her Camry, bleary-eyed but trying to hide it with a fake smile.

Tessa handed me an iced latte. "For you."

"Aw, thanks."

"So what's the latest on your aunt? She getting out soon?"

"I think so. She told me probably today."

I filled her in on the concussion thing, which she knew something about because her little brother, Logan, had ended up in the ER when he hit his head a few weeks ago. She'd done her research since.

"I'm surprised she didn't come home yesterday," Tessa said.

"I guess her concussion showed signs of being more serious, so they wanted to keep her overnight."

"Oh."

I stared out the window and sipped the drink. I couldn't meet Tessa's eyes. She had no idea what was going on with me, but I didn't want to test the depth of her sensitivities and see if she picked up on the turmoil. It was time to try out the skills I'd learned in theater class and act like I was fine. Maybe she'd think I was just upset over Aunt Laura. I didn't have to fake that.

"If something bad had to happen to Aunt Laura, why did it have to be a car accident?" I said as Tessa drove us to the barn.

"I'm so sorry," Tessa said.

"Guy ran a red light."

Tessa slowed at an intersection. "This is super tough, but we've also got to focus on the positive. Your aunt's okay. It could have been a whole lot worse."

"Yeah."

"I'm not saying that to discount your feelings, though," Tessa said. "There's been a lot going on for you this summer, right?"

I let out a sarcastic laugh. "You have no idea."

"I'd like to," Tessa said. "I'm sorry we haven't hung out like I thought we would."

"Yeah, things haven't exactly gone as planned for any of us, have they?"

She laughed, but it sounded real for her. "I'm barely recovered from Dad's wedding!"

I wondered what my life would've been like if my father had remarried and there were a stepmother in my life. Tessa's stepmom, Rebecca, hadn't exactly welcomed her with open arms. They were civil with each other, but that was likely as far as it would ever go.

It made sense. Her dad made some stupid choices, and the consequences included losing a lot of the closeness he'd had with Tessa.

"You could teach me something about getting through hard stuff," I said.

"Hah!"

"No, really. I don't know how you've managed."

"For one, friends like you." Tessa smiled at me. "And Izzy, and Amelia, and Alex."

Yeah, Alex was one of the good guys. When the going got tough, he hadn't abandoned Tessa like her dad. He'd been a real friend, not just a boyfriend. "And Mom has been there too." Tessa chuckled. "And a whole lot of therapy! I'm going to have to invite Kendra to my future wedding at this rate!"

"Don't you find it hard to talk about your feelings with a complete stranger?"

We were at the edge of town now, and the houses were more spread out. I still couldn't look directly at her.

"It was tough at first," Tessa said. "But I was kind of desperate."

I remembered when the social worker suggested to my grandmother that they get therapy for me, and Grams had adamantly refused. She was of a generation that looked down on people going to a therapist. Maybe it felt like a blot on her family name. Or on her.

"Are you sure you're okay?" Tessa asked. "I'm worried about you."

I almost cried just because she cared enough to ask, and I could see she was genuinely worried. But I couldn't think of any way to tell her what else was going on with me. Especially when I barely understood it myself.

"If you ever need to talk, I'm here."

"I'll just be glad when Aunt Laura's back" was all I said.

—◊—

I walked into the barn with Tessa, who at least wore sneakers today instead of flip-flops. The sight of the horses helped calm me. Something about their big, soft eyes and long faces always had a way of making things a little better.

"Sky's the only one you've met," I said, taking her down to the end of the barn.

Tessa peeked in on the mare. "Is something wrong with her leg?"

"What?" I quickly joined her at Sky's door.

Tessa pointed at the mare's back leg. It was cocked, and her eyes were closed.

"Oh. No, they do that when they're napping or resting."

I introduced her to Tank, the massive black horse, and he came right over to us, nearly knocking us over with his head nudging. I hadn't been able to tell if he was begging for treats or if this was his way of saying hello, but he could give someone a bloody nose if he hit them wrong.

Blaze made Tessa laugh when he nuzzled her neck, tickling her.

"His whiskers," she said.

"Yep."

"So . . ." Tessa turned toward me. "Izzy has been lobbying for me to talk you into letting us ride the horses."

I groaned. "Izzy!"

"I know, I know." Tessa held up her hands. "I'm just sayin'."

I lowered my voice. "I barely know these people."

"Well, it's time we change that," someone said behind us, and I turned to see Denise. She chuckled when she saw our embarrassed expressions.

"Sorry, couldn't help but overhear," she said, sticking out her hand toward my friend. "I'm Denise. I know we've met before, but I'm sorry I've forgotten your name. You are . . ."

"Tessa."

"I hope it was okay to bring her," I said, waiting for the verbal onslaught that Janie might've given me about respecting the farm's privacy and never bringing anyone without permission. I honestly hadn't been thinking about any of that. I needed to get out of the apartment, and Tessa offered me the lifeline.

"Of course," Denise said. "Did I hear you say you have a friend who wants to ride?"

"Um, that's an understatement," I said.

Denise tapped her nose, thinking. "I'll tell you what, Shay. I've been wanting to take some of our boys out on the trail around the property—get them familiar with it. Why don't you bring your friends, and we can make it a group."

I turned to Tessa. "Have you ever ridden a horse?"

"That would be a no," she said.

"Izzy has, but I'm not sure about Amelia."

Denise didn't seem fazed by this info. "That's okay. I've got a few Steady Eddies who can carry anyone. So, there are four of you? And I know you've ridden before, right?"

I realized the question was directed at me. I started to stammer something, but Tessa interrupted me. She grabbed hold of my arm. "Yes, Shay will do anything but speak highly of herself, so don't believe her if she says she doesn't have horse experience. She can ride better than any of us."

I blushed at the compliment and glanced at my feet. Then I looked up. "That's not really saying much, is it?"

Tessa threw back her head and laughed. "I guess not."

"Then why don't you girls come over tomorrow or the next day, and we'll hit the trail. Sound good?"

I didn't have to think twice. When Denise left us to organize the tack room, Tessa grinned. "Izzy is going to pee her pants! Let's text her now."

I pulled out my phone. "What should we say?"

"Here." Tessa sidled up next to me and took a fast selfie with me in front of Tank's stall. The horse poked his head over my shoulder right as she snapped it.

"Perfect!" she said.

She tapped out a caption: Shay and I are at Second Chance Farm. Guess what we just found out?

She sent the image to Amelia and Izzy.

We waited for them to get it. In a few seconds, Izzy replied: Oooooo! Cute horsie!!!

Amelia: What did you find???

"Go ahead," Tessa said. "You tell."

Me: We're all going on a trail ride!!!!

Izzy: OH MY STARS! Are you serious?

Tessa: Yep!

Izzy: For real?

Me: LOL

Izzy: *squeals and jumps around chaotically*

Tessa and I looked at each other, then laughed.

"Uh, you were right," I said.

"Did you doubt me?"

Izzy: *accidentally knocks over lamp while still squealing*

Amelia: I'm too heavy for a horse.

Uh-oh. I hadn't thought of that. She was self-conscious enough about her weight without this exclusion that would certainly be embarrassing. If she was past any of the horses' carrying limits, Amelia would be devastated, but she'd probably pretend it was nothing. Generally, a horse could carry 20 percent of its body weight, max, including tack. I didn't know how much Amelia weighed, but she didn't fall into the category of supremely overweight.

"What do I say?" I asked Tessa, whose fingers hovered over her own phone.

She typed, then turned the phone for me to read: Lady here will figure it out. It'll be fun! Don't worry!!

"Good?" Tessa asked.

I nodded. I just hoped it was true.

Another text came in, and it took me a second to realize it was from Aunt Laura.

"What?" Tessa leaned over. "By your smile, I guess that's good news?"

I couldn't help my grin. "She's coming home!"

Chapter
30

"SHAY, I CAN WALK BY MYSELF."

"I don't care," I said, practically gluing myself to my aunt's side as she climbed the steep stairs to the apartment.

We both laughed. She was walking pretty well. But I stayed alongside her because I desperately wanted a moment of lightness in the otherwise disturbing experience. Aunt Laura had waved off Ginny's help too. Ginny rolled her eyes and shook her head behind my aunt's back. We were both used to my aunt's independent streak.

"She's all yours!" Ginny had said. Aunt Laura had thrown her a pretend glare.

"I'm fine, I'm fine," Aunt Laura told me now at each step.

"You lie," I said, watching her wince and noticing the faint dullness in her eyes that signified pain. The hospital had sent her home with a bag of pills and discharge instructions that I'd tried to read, but Aunt Laura stuffed them into her pocket before I could.

"Stop being a worrywart," she said. "It's nothing a little rest and Netflix won't cure."

When she opened the door, Stanley about knocked her over. He wiggled and whined and ran to get his stuffed toy for her to throw. Aunt Laura slowly knelt on the floor and gave him a good greeting.

"He missed you," I said. "We all did."

"It was probably nice to have the place to yourself for a day, right?"

"Not exactly."

Aunt Laura carefully clambered back to her feet, waving me away when I went to help. "Seriously," she said. "Don't baby me."

What I really wanted to do was burst into tears and tell her how scared I had been and how I never wanted to leave her side, but I figured that would probably overwhelm her and make me feel foolish. I also wanted to grill her on what the doctors had said, but apparently "It was a concussion and I'll be fine" was all I was going to get. I resorted to at least making sure she had as many pillows and blankets on the sofa as possible, even if it was summer.

Aunt Laura sank onto the cushions with a groan of approval. "Oh, that feels good," she said. "I didn't sleep a wink last night."

I had started to sink down beside her, but I quickly got back up. "Okay, I won't bother you."

"No, no, no, Shay." Aunt Laura reached for my hand to keep me from leaving. "Sit. Stay."

I tried to hold back a smile but couldn't.

"What?"

"Sit? Stay?" I pointed at Stanley, who'd jumped up and now lay sprawled on the end of the sofa.

Aunt Laura chuckled. "Brain fog, meds, and sleep deprivation. Great combo."

I dropped to the sofa. I was exhausted too, and we sat for a moment in silence. Well, silent except for the rattling of the air-conditioning unit. *Thank you, God, for this,* I whispered in my heart. It was the first time I'd done anything close to praying in days, even though my friends had encouraged me otherwise.

"Is the Jeep totaled?" I asked.

Aunt Laura sighed. "I'm still waiting to hear from insurance."

I let another minute pass and waited for my aunt to speak. She was the one who'd been hurt, but how could I explain that I felt injured on the inside? Yet it didn't seem right to voice that out loud since she was the one in actual, physical pain and dealing now with hospital bills and car repairs. How was she going to pay for all that? Would she have to sell the store? Would we have to move? Would I have to go live with my grandparents again? I was only now starting to figure out how to make being here work. How would I—

"Hey." Aunt Laura patted my leg. "I see that look, kid."

"What look?"

"You're worrying."

I rested my head on the back of the sofa and looked at the ceiling, keeping the tears back. "You could've died!"

"True, Shay. But that's a possibility for everyone every day." She shifted her weight and grimaced. "Not to be morbid, but we can't live our lives wrapped in bubble wrap. I'm still here, alive and kicking. I did not die, and I'm not planning to anytime soon."

That sounded great, but it wasn't like someone could will away their death. I'm sure my dad wanted to stay here with me too, but he hadn't exactly had a choice.

"I realize how scary it must've been for you."

"Not your fault," I said, turning to look at her.

"No, but I keep asking myself all these questions. What if I'd been paying more attention? Or decided to go down Fifth Street instead of King? Or left ten minutes earlier—or later? I could go endlessly down that road too, Shay, but I will drive myself crazy doing that. Same as you will if you can't stop that busy little brain of yours from churning."

I rolled my eyes, and Aunt Laura laughed.

"Tall order, huh?" she said.

"Yeah."

"It's important to try, though." My aunt stuffed another pillow behind her back. "Look, I'm not an expert on God, but I know it's not His will that we hold on to everything ourselves. I do it too, but in my heart, I know He wants me to give things to Him far sooner than I usually do."

"You worry sometimes too?"

She nodded. "A lot. Hasn't helped that I have a teen girl under my roof who I really care about."

I shook my head. "I'm sorry I worry you."

My aunt bumped me with her shoulder. "That is not what I meant."

"I feel like I mess up all the time."

"Join the club."

"And sometimes it feels like nothing goes right."

"Yep," my aunt said. "Not to get all cynical on you, but I think that's called life, kiddo."

I was suddenly overcome with the need to be physically closer to her. When I first came here, personal space was important to both of us as we learned the rhythm of how to live together. But a life-and-death scare had a way of changing things, pushing them along.

For once, I tried not to overthink. I scooted closer to her and rested my head on her shoulder. I hoped she didn't mind.

"I thought things get easier as you get older," I said.

"Oh, I wish," she said with a snort. "I don't think 'easy' is a part of real life. It's nearly always complicated."

Complicated. She had that right. But as we rested on the sofa, one thing became clearer. I definitely wasn't going to the cottage with my grandparents. My aunt was going to need my help around the shop.

For now, I'd have to think about making dinner. And walking Stanley. I'd also need to coordinate with my friends about our trail ride and maybe text Zoe again since she hadn't gotten back to me. But in that moment, I realized everything could wait. At least for a little bit. There were a lot of things wrong in my world, but for a second at least, leaning against my very alive aunt, something felt incredibly right.

Chapter
31

Aunt Laura fell asleep on the sofa before dinner, and I let her doze. I could reheat the macaroni and cheese I'd made if she was hungry, but I had a feeling she would be out for a while. I walked and fed Stanley, and then he returned to the sofa and curled up on Aunt Laura's legs. Matilda hadn't moved from the back of the sofa cushions. I tiptoed over and snapped a picture of the threesome and texted it to the girls with a heart emoji and the word *Family*.

Izzy: Aww! So cute! ♥

Tessa: So glad she's home.

Amelia: Adorable!

Izzy: I'm SO looking forward to Friday!

We'd arranged with Denise to do our trail ride two days from now so I could feel better about leaving Aunt Laura. Izzy was intent on planning a picnic lunch and needed the time to get the supplies anyway.

I updated my grandmother briefly via text, even though she

didn't text much. I didn't think I could talk to her on the phone right now—or generally ever.

All I got back was a thank-you, which I guess was better than nothing. Grams had been there for me at least a little bit when she'd dropped everything to take me to the hospital.

I sent another text to Zoe, asking her to ignore the one I'd sent her the other night, but that was probably a stupid idea because it was only bringing to her attention the fact that I'd contacted her at all.

Sure enough, a few minutes later a new text from her popped up on my phone.

Zoe: I'm so sorry I missed your other text!

Me: No worries.

Zoe: Have time to talk now?

I was lying on my back in my pajamas in my bedroom. Oh, I was extremely busy and had no time.

Me: I guess so.

Zoe: You asked why God allows suffering.

Me: Yeah, but it's okay. You don't need to answer.

Zoe: It's a good question.

Was it? Maybe. Certainly a question many people asked but few could answer.

Me: What do u think?

There was a good thirty-second pause in the exchange, enough time for me to reconsider my choice to contact this woman. I'd asked Tessa if it was uncomfortable for her to spill her heart to a stranger, and even though Zoe was a little more than that to me, it wasn't by much. Yet maybe in some ways, that's what made things easier. Because she *didn't* really know me, there weren't the usual worries of what she might think of me. Sure, she could probably tell my aunt about stuff if she wanted because that was part of her job working with teenagers, but there was no real risk on my part. She wasn't a friend who wouldn't speak to me if I said something stupid, or a kid from school who'd give me weird looks in the halls or spread rumors—or truths—about me via social media.

Zoe: I think God COULD HAVE "forced" us to love Him and obey Him. He could have made it so we didn't have a choice in anything.

Me: Because He's God.

Zoe: Right. But He didn't. He died for us, loved us, set us up for success . . . but then He leaves the choice up to us whether we're gonna receive or not. Walk in His ways or not.

Me: 'Cuz we'd be robots otherwise.

Zoe: Yeah. Where would the beauty be in that?

Me: Being a robot might be kinda nice sometimes, LOL.

Zoe: Haha!! You're right. I feel the same way. But ultimately, there is greater joy knowing we are loved for who we are, even as broken people.

Me: I guess that makes sense.

Zoe: I think the Bible makes it clear that suffering comes from the fact that everyone is allowed to make their own choices. And because we're all sinners, we often make stupid choices—things God doesn't want us to do because He knows they will harm us. But He allows us to because He didn't want to have robots as His children any more than you might want to have a horse with zero personality that's dull to the world and always does everything you want it to do.

That was speaking my language. In some of the online training videos I'd watched, the horses were clearly doing things because they didn't feel like they had a choice. I always felt bad for them.

Me: I still wish some people didn't have a choice. Like people who use their choices to hurt others on purpose.

Zoe: Yeah, I know. Living in a fallen world is confusing and complicated. How are you doing with everything?

Me: OK. Thanks.

Zoe: Summer going any better?

Me: A little.

Zoe: That's good!

I wasn't up for expanding on those thoughts. I said goodbye and rested my phone on my chest. The other night I'd taken my chance to make good choices and blown it. *Squandered your resources*, Grams would say.

Before I went to bed, I checked on my aunt. She was still sound asleep on the couch, a slight snore rumbling from her. I went back into my room, took my mom's journal from the drawer, and placed it on the coffee table beside the sofa where my aunt would see it when she woke up. On a Post-it Note I wrote, *I can't read any more so I wanted you to have this.*

Chapter

32

I'D HOPED THINGS WOULD LOOK CLEARER after a good night's sleep. Except I didn't *get* a good night's sleep. My air-conditioning unit still wasn't cooling the room enough, and I woke up at one o'clock, sweating. For an hour I tried to go back to sleep, but nothing worked. So I picked up my phone to scroll through my limited social media apps. I still wasn't sleepy enough. A little voice nagged at me, urging me to go back to what I'd seen the other night—and I listened.

Again.

Only this time, I didn't have any excuses. My aunt was home and safe and alive. The other night, I could've chalked it up to stress and the unknown, or a huge mistake I'd made that I'd repented of and moved away from.

After I skimmed through web pages, filling my mind with those pictures once again, I put the phone down, disgusted with myself. But it didn't end there. The dreams I had afterward filled me with guilt and shame once I woke up. What kind of a girl was I?

I rolled over and buried my head in my pillow. *Oh, Lord, I'm sorry. I don't know why I'm doing this. I don't know how to stop.*

A sharp knock came at my door.

"Come in," I said.

Aunt Laura poked her head inside. She held a steaming coffee cup, and I wondered how she could drink anything hot in the middle of summer.

"Good morning, sleepyhead," she said, her voice all chipper, like she'd never had a concussion and had the best sleep ever.

"How are you feeling?" I asked.

"Better than you look."

"I just woke up!"

Or more accurately, I hardly slept.

She laughed. "Don't be mad at me, but I'm going down to do a little work in the store."

"But didn't the doctor say . . . ?"

"Nothing strenuous, I promise."

I threw her a look, but there was no arguing with her. "What time is it?"

"Seven."

I grabbed my pillow and held it over my head, muffling my protests. Maybe I had slept more than a few minutes after all.

Enveloped in brain fog, I dressed, ate a bowl of raisin bran, and took Stanley for a walk to Founder's Park, thinking that might wake me up. It was early enough that the sun hadn't created a sauna yet, but I still wished I'd worn a sleeveless T-shirt. I passed joggers, walkers, and fellow "dog people." I watched for Abraham and his dog, hoping I would run into them.

As I passed Grounds and Rounds, I thought of Zoe and our text conversation. I half expected her to be outside again, talking with more kids. But that was silly. She had a life that probably went far beyond her youth ministry work.

My phone vibrated, and I checked it.

Izzy: How is your aunt?

Me: Home. She's okay.

Izzy: I've been praying for both of you. ♥

Me: Thank you.

Izzy: If you need anything, let me know!

Me: Ok.

Izzy: Seriously! Tell me.

Hmm. Cupcakes. Could I tell her we needed cupcakes? I had visions of vanilla with some sort of strawberry frosting, but I kept that to myself.

Me: ♥ Thanks, Izzy. Appreciate you.

I hadn't realized how much I'd missed her when she went mute on me, but it sure felt good to have her back.

I squinted at my screen, barely able to see it in the sunshine.

Izzy: I can't wait for Friday!!!

Me: Me either!

In all the darkness, there was no greater light than friends and being on the back of a horse. And on Friday, I would get both.

—◊—

I did not get the horse I'd expected.

I stared at the Haflinger, then at Denise, and then back at the Haflinger. Haflingers are a short breed and look like miniature draft horses, with golden chestnut bodies and flaxen manes, but this one was smaller than any I'd ever seen.

"His name is Strudel," Denise said.

Izzy immediately started giggling from behind me. "He's adorbs!"

Tessa had picked me up at the bookstore at seven thirty with Izzy and Amelia already in tow. We were trying to beat some of the day's heat and get out on the horses early.

Denise had met us in the barn and assigned us our steeds, as she called them.

I was right about Amelia. She'd protested about riding in general, never giving the reason—except I knew, and I suspected Denise did too. Denise hadn't batted an eye as she opened the door to Tank's stall and handed his lead rope to Amelia. Amelia was immediately smitten. My friend started baby-talking that big horse and brushing him out like she'd grown up doing it.

Izzy got Blaze, Tessa got Sky, and then it was my turn.

Strudel couldn't have been more than 13 hands tall.

"He's sturdier than he looks," Denise said.

I mean, Izzy was right about how cute he was, but I'd had visions of cantering off in a field. Those visions quickly disintegrated when I saw Strudel's stubby little legs.

"He needs the most experienced rider," Denise said. "That's you."

"Experienced?" Did five lessons and a dozen trail rides make me experienced?

"Oh, don't worry, he's safe." She laughed and handed me his plastic tote grooming box stuffed with multiple brushes, currycombs, and a hoof pick.

"When we first got him, he had a lot of trust issues and would get stressed over seemingly little things." Denise picked up a currycomb and started brushing him. Dust swirled into the air, evidence he'd had a good roll recently. Good thing none of us had allergies.

"It took him a while to open up, but we went slow."

"What do you mean 'trust issues'?" I asked.

The older woman rubbed the brush firmly across Strudel's rump, and I started brushing him on the opposite side. "His previous owner used some harsh training methods. Strudel learned that people can't always be trusted. Haflingers are super smart, and this guy's very sensitive."

I glanced over at Tessa. She stared down at her hand, now coated with dust. "Ew," she whispered, and I laughed.

Izzy found a spot on Blaze's neck that he apparently liked, and when she scratched him, he raised his head and leaned into it. Amelia was now singing softly to Tank, who stood there like a stone wall.

It took us twenty minutes to get the horses brushed and their hooves picked of any dirt and stones they'd gathered in the fields overnight. Denise handed out helmets for everyone and helped us make sure our western saddles were all secure, with their cinches pulled tight. I knew how to bridle a horse and managed Strudel's, but the other girls were clueless.

"This is amazing," Izzy leaned toward me and whispered once we were heading out to the arena to mount. "Thank you so much!"

"Wasn't me, but you're welcome," I said.

Denise was riding another black horse named Mack that looked like Tank but without the white blaze on his face.

It was quite the undertaking, getting us girls in the saddle. I felt myself growing impatient as my well-meaning but clueless-about-horses friends tried to mount. The farm had a mounting block, which was just a plastic stool with a couple of steps. Denise was in no hurry and took her time with each girl.

Izzy was practically bouncing on her toes when her turn came, and Denise was smiling. I think she liked the enthusiasm.

"Put your foot in the stirrup there," Denise said.

Izzy obeyed, but before Denise could get out any further instruction, Izzy hoisted herself up to the saddle with much more force than needed, and she went flying over the other side and landed in a heap in the sandy arena.

Amelia burst into laughter, then stopped when she realized neither I nor Denise was laughing.

I jumped off Strudel—it wasn't a big leap—and rushed over to Izzy. "Are you okay?"

Izzy popped onto her feet. "I'm good!"

I tried to brush the sand off the side of her jeans, but she didn't seem to care.

"Let's try that again, shall we?" Denise smiled again once she saw that Izzy wasn't hurt.

By the time we were all in the saddle and Denise instructed the girls on the basics of steering inside the arena, the sun had risen higher in the sky. The day wasn't as hot as it could've been, but our ride wasn't going to be the long, relaxing adventure I'd hoped. Oh well. My friends probably couldn't handle a long trail ride anyway.

"Are you girls ready?" Denise called over her shoulder as she opened the arena gate from atop her horse like a legit cowgirl. She was the only one of us not wearing a helmet, instead topping her head with a straw cowboy hat. I figured she knew what she was doing, but it still made me a little nervous.

"Yes!" Izzy raised herself a bit in her saddle, and I noticed Blaze pin his ears, a sure sign he wasn't liking something.

"So, we want to keep our movements quiet while we're on these horses' backs," Denise said. "They can feel a fly when it lands on their skin, so they can sense our every movement on their backs. Let's be conscious of that."

Amelia raised her hand.

"Yes?"

"Are we going to gallop?"

I held in a laugh. Beginners do not gallop horses.

"Not today," Denise said.

Izzy turned toward me. "Have you ever galloped?"

I shook my head. Life Goals No. 1, though.

Denise took the lead on Mack, and we were off. The "trail" on the property wasn't much more than a narrow, worn dirt path. I'd walked it a few times for fun after work when I started with Janie. It would make a good first experience for the others.

Strudel kept up far better than I had expected. If anything, I needed to continually slow him down.

"He loves to hang out with his friends," Denise said when she saw me holding my reins tight. "Give him a little slack in those reins if you can. This is where *you* have to trust, as hard as that is. If we hold the reins too tightly, the horses can feel anxious. Plus, they need to be able to move their heads should they take a wrong step."

Why did so much seem to be about trust with these horses?

"You girls are Christians?" Denise asked.

"Yes!" Izzy exclaimed. She was right behind Denise, then Amelia and Tessa, and I was bringing up the rear.

"I love the analogies horses give us for our relationship with God," Denise said. "We have to trust Him, too, right? And that's not always easy, but it's as necessary as breathing."

Oh boy. How badly was I letting God down by struggling so much in the trust area?

We walked the horses for about ten minutes along the fence line surrounding the property, and I tried to simply breathe and enjoy the moment. Strudel was steady enough, but I could feel his body tense every now and again if he heard something in the tall grasses or a leaf blew across the path.

"You doing okay back there?"

I gave Denise a wave, hoping I didn't look nervous. I couldn't deny I wanted my friends to see I knew something about horses through all this—and maybe impress them a teeny bit if I could. I'd worked hard to gain the knowledge I had.

Strudel kept trying to get ahead of the others, and I kept pulling on his reins to stop him. I'd been trying to do what Denise said and give him some rein, but he felt like he was going to start running if I did that.

Glancing back at us, Denise gestured for me to come up. "It's okay if you want to switch order or walk side by side for a bit," she said. "They all get along for the most part."

I chuckled. "For the most part?"

"They have spats too, like all of us," Denise said.

"Oh, we know about spats," Amelia said. I wondered if she was referring to when she and Tessa had been nearly at each other's throats over some misunderstandings a few weeks back, most notably when Amelia told Tessa that Alex was breaking up with her when he had planned no such thing. Amelia had meant well and was only trying to protect Tessa's feelings, but it still created a huge issue in Tessa's heart as it dredged up past hurts and disappointments from her father.

I let Strudel go a little, and he walked briskly to come alongside Sky and Tessa.

"Hey," I said. "Fancy seeing you riding a horse!"

Tessa was grinning. "I never would've thought you'd talk me into this."

"But it's fun, right?"

"I'll give you that."

Amelia had made her way up to the front of the line and was chatting away with Denise. I heard the words *musical* and *Annie* and figured the woman was getting an earful about Amelia's passion.

"I've actually been wanting to talk to you," Tessa said.

"Well, here I am!" I held out one arm to indicate I was wide open.

We passed a junkyard full of cars in various states of disrepair. Some looked like they could be started and driven off the property; others were rusted through and would be better off scrapped entirely.

"Are you okay?"

My pulse jumped a little at the question. "Uh, yeah, sure."

"Really?" Tessa gave me a concerned look that made my heart hurt. She genuinely cared about me.

"I mean, things haven't been easy," I said.

"I know," Tessa said. "But it seems like you haven't been honest with me lately."

The way she said it wasn't mean or judgmental. It was surprisingly sad.

"We don't have to talk now, but maybe later?" she asked.

My throat tightened. "Okay."

"I care about you," Tessa said. "We all do."

"I know," I nearly whispered.

"You can tell me anything, and I'm not going anywhere."

That was an easy thing to say when you didn't know what your friend was doing in the middle of the night. But Tessa had stood by me at my lowest last year. She was the first one I told about my experience in juvie, and she hadn't reacted at all like I'd expected. She'd just loved on me and embraced me, giving me exactly the support I'd needed to be able to get through. Izzy and Amelia had too, once they'd understood the depth of what I was going through.

Tessa held her reins like the beginner she was—tightly, her arms stiff and locked. "I mean that," Tessa said.

Izzy turned around and beamed back at me, her pink cowboy boots fitting right in against Blaze's blingy saddle. Apparently his previous owner had donated her barrel-racing tack, and this saddle was all turquoise and silver. "What are you two talking about?"

"Um . . . nothing," I said, unable to look at Tessa. I squeezed Strudel's sides with my calves. He surged forward to Izzy, and Tessa brought Sky along the other side.

"Having fun?" I asked Izzy. Based on the sunshine that seemed to radiate from her face, I could guess the answer.

"Oh goodness, yes," she said. "I could live right here in this saddle."

I glanced at Tessa, and she gently smiled at me. I did not want to lie to her or anyone, but I didn't need to tell anyone anything either. It was private. Between me and God. Right?

Chapter

33

I COULD'VE STAYED ON THE BACK OF A HORSE for the rest of the day, enjoying the rhythmic thumping of hooves on the packed dirt, inhaling the scent of fresh cut grass and sweaty equine, and relishing having my friends by my side. *This* was how I had envisioned summer. And I wanted to hold on to it as long as I could.

"I'm famished," Izzy exclaimed after we'd all dismounted at the three green picnic tables at the edge of the property.

"Me too!" Amelia echoed.

Each of the horses wore rope halters and lead ropes under their bridles, so once we removed the bridles, they could be tied to the highline Denise set up between two small trees. The older woman took care of the horses while we girls sat down at one of the picnic tables and unpacked our lunches from Tank's saddle bags. We'd stashed our phones in there too, and I pulled mine out and set it on the table. My mind flashed back to school and how we'd eat together in the cafeteria almost every single day—the Riverbend friends who were more the same than different. If we hurt each other, we eventually made up. If one of us struggled, the others gathered around and were strong when our friend was weak. At least, that's how it worked in theory. I hadn't been there for Tessa like I'd wanted to when she was dealing with her parents' messy divorce. I always felt so clumsy in friendship. By the time I figured out a way to be a true friend, the moment had passed.

We prayed over our food, and Denise took hers to sit with the horses and make a few business calls. I wouldn't have minded her company, but I think she wanted the outing to be a girls' day for us.

"I've been thinking about contacting my father," I said.

The statement was probably somewhat of a surprise to Izzy and Amelia, but for me, it was the culmination of my thoughts about him over the past few weeks.

Izzy paused with her sandwich halfway to her mouth. "Whoa, really?"

"I have an e-mail ready to go."

Tessa crunched on a carrot stick. "I wasn't sure how serious you were."

"I wasn't sure either, but I think I want to."

Amelia's eyes got big like a Boston terrier's. She chugged down a few gulps of her Dr Pepper and wiped her mouth with her napkin. "But I thought you were done with him."

She was right. I had been. After that terrible horse clinic, I'd sworn off anything to do with Mason King.

"Yeah," Izzy said. "You stopped watching his videos and everything."

I tore my sandwich in half. "I kinda started watching them again."

"Why?" Izzy asked.

"I mean, he is my father." I took a bite of the chicken salad goodness.

"Who was a jerk," Izzy said.

"True." I hadn't forgotten how he'd treated Ava, or how scared she'd been when he'd whipped her, but I was maybe willing to look past that, at least temporarily, to learn more about him. "But I'm curious. He *is* half my DNA."

Amelia grabbed my phone. I didn't have a passcode on it like the other girls did on theirs, so we often used mine to look things up on Google.

"What's his website again?" Amelia asked.

I rattled it off to her, and she started tapping at the screen.

"Ew!" Amelia threw the phone across the table as if it had bitten her. "What was *that*?"

"What was what?" Izzy picked up the phone and stared at the screen, her face shifting to disgust.

I tried to grab it away from her, but Izzy stood and held my phone under Tessa's nose so she, too, could see whatever was causing them both to react.

I suddenly felt like throwing up.

Oh, dear God, what have they seen?

Then Izzy shoved the phone in my face. "Why is this on your phone?"

The photo on the screen was something I wished I had never seen before. It depicted a man and a woman doing something only married people should do, with nothing left to the imagination. One of the images I'd been looking at the last time I had my Internet browser open was still there.

I glanced at Tessa, and she gave me that same sad expression I'd seen earlier, like she'd already known. I *could* deny any knowledge of the picture. Weird stuff happened with phones all the time. I could say I'd accidentally clicked on an e-mail attachment that took me to an inappropriate site. I could claim I'd been as horrified then as my friends were now, but that the browser still remembered.

I was pretty sure they'd believe me.

But *I* would know. How could I expect to have deep, meaningful friendships built on lies?

"It's not what you—" I started to do it, to tell my friends a flat-out falsehood because I was ashamed. And I didn't want to face the reality that they might abandon me when I needed them most.

"Shay, tell us the truth. Were you looking at this stuff?" Amelia said, her voice strong and insistent.

I stared at the splintered wood of the picnic table, then tried to meet each of their eyes. I couldn't speak. How could I possibly tell them what I'd done?

Tessa was sitting across from me, and she leaned forward. "The other night when I was at your house, I dropped my phone on the floor. When I went to pick it up, I saw that book under your bed. That's what I wanted to talk to you about later. I didn't realize there was other . . . stuff."

"So, wait." Izzy's eyes held a fury I'd never seen before. I wanted to scoot down the bench away from her. "You didn't answer Amelia."

I swallowed hard. I had avoided the question, but how *could* I answer?

"Obviously she was looking at it," Amelia said in disgust. "It's her phone."

"I was just . . . curious," I whispered.

"About what, sex?"

I cringed at the way Amelia said it so boldly.

Where was Denise? Would she come over and rescue me from this conversation?

"If I'm being honest, yes!"

Izzy pushed my phone as far away as she could, probably scratching the screen on the rough wood as she did so. "This is pornography!"

At the mention of that word, I felt my world collapse. Everything I'd been holding in pushed through the cracks and annihilated the defenses I'd built up to deny what I'd been doing.

Tessa spoke in a soft voice. "You seriously were looking at this stuff?"

"I . . . it wasn't a lot."

"Oh my gosh, why?" Izzy hadn't lowered her voice at all.

Could I say I didn't know? That I'd gotten frustrated and curious and defiant, and I made some stupid decisions?

"When did this start?" Tessa asked.

I clenched my hands together and glanced at the horses. All of them were calmly eating grass, clueless about the drama unfolding between four teenage girls, one of whom was watching her friendships crumble before her eyes.

"It hasn't been long," I said.

"So you *are* reading those books." Tessa wasn't asking a question. "And looking at these pictures."

"Some," I said. I could feel heat creeping up my neck.

"Oh, Shay."

"I knew I shouldn't," I said lamely, picking at a splinter on the table so I didn't have to see their expressions.

Izzy crumpled up her oily cookie bag. "Are you kidding me?"

"Guys, I'm sorry."

"It hurts you more than it hurts us," Tessa said.

When I looked at Izzy's face, I wasn't sure if she agreed.

"It hasn't been very long," I said again in a thin voice, feeling tears threatening to overflow. "I know I shouldn't have, but I was honestly curious."

"So you *searched* for naked pictures?" Izzy said. "On *purpose?*"

I couldn't acknowledge her. I just held my hand over my face.

"Shay?"

All I could do was nod.

Chapter
34

Izzy stepped away from me, throwing up her hands. "I'm sorry, but I can't talk to you right now."

Could I blame her? I sat there with my shoulders slumped. By this time, Denise had noticed our squabble and made her way over to us.

"What's wrong, girls?"

The fury on Izzy's face had caused her cheeks to redden. Was she going to blurt everything out to this woman we barely knew?

"Nothing," Izzy said sharply.

Denise looked at my other friends, and they just stared at Izzy and me.

"We're just . . . talking," Tessa said.

"Looked like a bit more than that."

"Friends have disagreements sometimes," Izzy said. She picked up the rest of her lunch and took it to the second picnic table.

I understood her disappointment, but it hurt more than I'd

expected. Obviously, I wasn't proud of any of this either. I knew what I did was wrong just as much as they did. But I also didn't know what to do about it, and I'd hoped my friends could help.

Amelia seemed torn between following Izzy and staying with me. She and Izzy had similar mindsets in some ways, kind of like Tessa and I did. Amelia always wanted everything to go as planned, in a specific order, in life and in theater. Izzy was more spontaneous, but they both shared a zest for life that I seemed to always be chasing.

Finally, Amelia grabbed her own lunch. "Sorry," she whispered and walked over to sit with Izzy.

Tessa crossed her arms and leaned toward me. "This is a big deal," she said.

"I know!" It was my turn to get up. I stomped over to the horses, and I saw Strudel jump in place.

"Easy there," Denise said.

"I don't want to talk about it."

"I didn't ask you to. I want you to be smart around the horses."

She was right. I stood still. "We'll figure it out. We always do," I said, but I was saying the words more to convince myself than as a statement of fact. And tears were coming whether I wanted them to or not.

Denise stood there, watching me. "That wasn't a simple disagreement, was it?"

I shook my head.

"Well, why don't you sit with these guys for a little bit." Denise patted Tank on the shoulder. He glanced back at her as if to check whether she was offering treats, then he returned to eating grass. Strudel was grazing too, but I could see him watching me out of the corner of his eye.

Should I try to talk to Izzy? Probably. But the embarrassment I was feeling prevented me from doing anything.

I sank to the grass beside the animals and let myself soak in their calm before I did anything. Maybe they'd give me the courage I needed to face my friends. My hands were shaking, and it was taking everything in me to hold back the tears.

It was one of the hardest things I'd done in a long time, but I got up and went over to the picnic table where Izzy, Amelia, and now Tessa sat.

I didn't try to sit with them, but I got close.

"I'm not expecting you to tell me it's okay," I said.

"Never would," Izzy muttered.

"Quiet," Tessa said, glancing up at me. "Let Shay talk." I wondered if there was any chance Tessa could at least understand that this wasn't who I really was.

Izzy was crying now, and I hadn't expected that.

"Don't you remember what happened with . . . me?" Izzy pleaded with her eyes for me to understand, and I didn't know what to say.

"What do you mean?" I asked her.

"You know what those guys did. Pornography is . . . it's evil. It objectifies and humiliates women. I thought you *knew* that. I thought you were my friend!"

I realized what she was talking about. The Dropbox scandal. Boys paying to view inappropriate photos.

"I *am* your friend," I said.

Amelia piped in. "Why would you even want to look at that stuff? You're a girl."

I had no answer for that. None that made sense, anyway. I felt like I'd been hit with a ball of fire—and every part of me was in pain. In one sense, I couldn't move. In another, I wanted to run.

I stepped back from the table while my friends kept talking. They were trying to process this situation together. That's what friends do. And some part of me wanted to be there with them, talking about it. Figuring it out. Making things better. But I found myself backing away, a small step at a time.

Denise had joined us, maybe trying to find out what the real deal was. Then, without asking permission, I grabbed my helmet and went to Strudel, quickly and quietly rebridling him. Without taking more time to think, I undid Strudel's lead rope, threw the reins over his head, and climbed onto his back. He was short enough that I didn't need a mounting block.

"Shay, what are you doing?" Denise called after me, but I ignored her.

I might not gallop, but I was going to do something my friends couldn't.

I was going to ride, and I was going to ride fast. Away.

Chapter
35

I'D MADE SOME STUPID DECISIONS in my short life, but getting on the back of Strudel, a horse I didn't know, and expecting to canter off into the sunset might've been the stupidest of them all. Or the bravest, depending on how you looked at it. I hadn't decided which it was when I encouraged Strudel into a trot down the trail despite Denise's calls for me to come back. I should've listened to her. Strudel was her horse, and if I expected to work at this barn, respecting the owner was kind of at the top of the to-do list.

The farther down the trail I got, the more I realized my decision was more stupid than brave. But my mind was hardly clear.

"Slow down, boy!" I said to the pony, who was increasing his speed with each stride, keeping pace with my ever-pounding heart. What should I have expected? My friends to be perfectly fine and tell me it was okay? It wasn't fine. I had sinned against God. And my friends had every right to point that out. Would they forgive me? Would God?

Strudel trotted faster. I pulled back on the reins.

Instead of slowing, he sped up.

We trotted down the grassy path, passing trees in a whirl.

Izzy was right. How *could* I?

Strudel's fast trot quickly turned into a canter, and I felt myself pitch forward. I tried to lean back like my instructor had told me at one of my lessons, and that helped a little, but he still went faster. Then I recalled something I should have remembered before starting this stupid, dramatic exit. Horses often run faster when heading back to their barns.

We neared the junkyard, and I started to freak out. I might be the most experienced rider of my friend group, but I wasn't used to cantering for an extended period of time. And most of my riding had been done in safe, enclosed rings, sometimes at the end of a lunge line controlled by the instructor. Not an open pasture or wooded path with scary objects along the way. I was so stupid. In so many ways.

I never should have read those novels.

Or read my mom's journal.

Or talked back to my grandmother.

Looked for my father.

Hit that girl.

Taken this horse.

My decisions lined up like dominoes, and all it took was a racing pony for them to come tumbling down. I couldn't see the barn from here, but Strudel knew exactly where he was going.

I thought I heard the faint sound of someone calling my name, but I couldn't be sure. Everything became a blur, and my focus was on nothing but hanging on.

I lost a stirrup, and it threw me off balance.

I didn't see the log in the middle of the path. I hadn't noticed it on the way out since the horses were walking and apparently had calmly stepped over it.

But Strudel saw it. And decided he wasn't going to jump it. With no time to think or prepare, he zigged and I zagged. One second, I was barreling down the path on a horse intent on getting home as fast as possible. And the next, I wasn't.

When I hit the ground, I hit hard. First my arm, and then my back, made contact. I couldn't breathe. Pain shot through my arm. I rolled over, trying to suck in air. Blue sky above me. No air in my lungs.

I gasped but couldn't pull in any oxygen. Something in the back of my mind told me I'd knocked the wind out of me, but the rest of my body flipped out. I thought I was going to die. Or be paralyzed. I'd never ride horses again. Another gasping attempt to live allowed a little air inside my lungs, and the darkness around my vision slowly cleared.

I rolled to my side and tried to sit up. Not so easy. I looked around. Strudel had literally left me in the dust. I lifted my right arm, and blood dripped onto the ground. It took me a second to figure out why. Then I saw the gash in my forearm, and I tried not to freak out even more. It looked deep, and blood was gushing out of the wound. Instinctively I covered the gash with my other hand, and soon more blood was dripping through my fingers.

Oh, Lord, how bad is this?

I was still sitting on the ground when I heard hoofbeats in the distance. For a brief moment, I thought maybe Strudel was coming back to me, but when I looked up, I saw Denise cantering Tank down the path toward me. They stopped a few feet away. She swung her leg over Tank's thick back and quickly dismounted. When she knelt down, I was still gasping.

"I'm . . . I'm sorry. I shouldn't have . . . taken him."

"Hey, hey." Denise gently peeled my fingers away from my arm. I couldn't look at the wound. "Just breathe."

"How bad?" I asked, wincing at the sting.

"It'll need stitches," Denise said. "Did you hit your head?"

"No, I don't think so."

"That's good."

My tears flowed like the blood from my wound. "I really messed up," I sobbed.

Denise glanced over her shoulder in the direction of the barn. "Okay, listen. First, we're going to get you back to the house."

"But Strudel—"

"Is probably already back at the barn," Denise said. She pulled a bandana from her pocket and wrapped it around my arm, which was shaking like the rest of my body.

"My friends," I said.

"They'll walk the other horses back. Can you stand?"

I wasn't sure if I could, but I tried anyway. Denise wrapped her arm around my back and supported me, and somehow I managed to get up.

"Do you feel dizzy?"

"No."

But the thought of walking all the way back to the barn made me feel like I was going to throw up.

"Let's get you on Tank," Denise said.

With her help, I climbed onto the back of the big black horse. He stood there like a boulder. Once I was settled, Tank turned his head and looked at me, almost like he was making sure I was okay.

For a second, we stood still, and I kept trying to breathe without gasping. Denise got on her phone and called Link, who said he'd come and help my friends get back to the barn safely. I wondered if they were even thinking about me. I felt like they would be happier right now without me anywhere nearby.

"Okay, that's good news," Denise said into the phone, then pocketed it. "Strudel ran right into his stall."

Well, at least I hadn't killed a pony.

"So, I don't think I have to tell you that was a really bad idea?"

"I'm so sorry." I gulped against the pain and nausea.

"You could've been killed."

Was that supposed to make me feel better?

Denise walked beside me and Tank as we plodded along. She led him by his reins, so all I had to do was focus on staying in the saddle. I could feel the bandana already soaking with blood, and soon it was dripping through, landing on my jeans and Tank's saddle.

"Your friends are worried," she said.

"And they're mad at me."

"Well, real friends stick with you. They might get mad, and you might not talk for a little bit, but most things can be worked out."

I wasn't so sure about that. I might've completely blown my chances. Would they ever treat me the same again? They certainly would never see me the same way again.

My left hand was coated with blood, my entire body hurt, and all of it mirrored how I felt on the inside. I'd been trying so hard to deal with things on my own, but I wasn't sure if I could even try anymore.

"They told me a little about what was going on," Denise said. Tank took us around a tree stump, and I held on to the saddle horn with my good hand. Where had my courage gone? Only a few minutes ago I'd jumped into the saddle, intent on speed. Now I felt like I was going to fall off at a walk. Maybe I *had* hit my head. Because the world seemed to be spinning around me.

"What did they say?" I asked.

"They're concerned, Shay." Denise looked up at me. "And all I can say is this: Don't wait until things are out of control before you talk to people, okay? We can help you find someone. Someone who's helped others."

Tank kept walking, and soon I could see the barn in the distance. An ATV barreled toward us on the path, and Link stopped to check on us before leaving to help my friends. Through it all, the horse didn't flinch, and neither did Denise. It seemed like it would take a heck of a lot for either of them to get worked up.

When we got to the barn, Denise helped me slowly slide out of the saddle and sit on a hay bale. She put Tank in the round pen, then rushed to get a first aid kit.

I closed my eyes and tried not to cry from the throbbing pain in my arm.

"Should I call your aunt?" Denise asked, unwrapping the bandana, now soaked through with my blood. She gave me a clean towel to hold over the wound.

"She's not allowed to drive right now and doesn't have a car anyway," I said.

I explained about her car accident and how she'd just gotten back from the hospital. Denise instantly switched gears and prepared to take me to urgent care herself. As she went to get their truck, I pulled out my phone. Weirdly, instead of calling Aunt Laura, I tried to send her a one-handed text even though I was still shaking. Maybe I thought a text wouldn't scare her as badly.

Me: **Fell off horse and cut my arm. Prob needs stitches. I'm fine but not sure what to do.**

Within a minute, my phone started ringing, and I picked up.

"Shay, are you okay?" My aunt's voice sounded frantic.

"I'm fine." I wondered how I had gotten so adept at lying.

"What happened?"

I didn't want to tell her all the details, but I gave her enough. Then I handed the phone to Denise, who had hopped out of the truck to get me. She and my aunt figured out the best place to take me and what to do about permissions, insurance, and stuff I didn't know anything about.

"Your niece is a tough cookie," Denise said with a smile at me.

Yeah, too tough sometimes.

Denise hung up and handed the phone back to me, and I felt a little better now that the grown-ups were taking charge. But when I heard the ATV in the distance, I was reminded that the truly tough stuff was just beginning.

Chapter
36

Each bump down the driveway made me wince. I could tell Denise wasn't going to *force* me to talk about anything, but I felt this huge weight of embarrassment over what I'd done with Strudel. And I wondered whether the girls had told her about the other stuff.

"Did my friends say why we were arguing?"

"They're quite concerned about you."

So that was a yes.

In some ways, it was a relief. I wouldn't have to say, *Oh, by the way, they're mad at me because I was looking at porn.* Even wording it like that in my head was embarrassing. I could feel my cheeks flush with shame. *Well, when feeling embarrassed, deflect!*

"I guess you probably don't want me to be around the horses anymore."

Denise chuckled. "The thought crossed my mind, but the truth is, I'm thinking now you probably need to be around them *more*."

Um, what was that supposed to mean?

"Shay, look. Let's be real. Janie told me a little bit about your situation, so I know things haven't been easy for you."

"She did?"

Denise nodded. "Our work with horses is about healing relationships and people as much as it is about rescuing animals. I could see how much you loved the horses here right from the beginning, and I want you to be a part of that with us too—if you want."

Denise turned the truck onto the road leading into Riverbend. The urgent care clinic was on the other side of town.

"I'm more interested in *you* and what you're going through right now. We can talk about Strudel later, because what you did was very dangerous. But thankfully he's okay, and you'll be okay once we stitch you up."

I cradled my arm. It throbbed, but she was right. I'd get some stitches and pain meds, and physically, I'd be okay. I wasn't sure how I would feel when it came to getting back on a horse, though. I'd heard about people who were forever scarred after a fall, like in that old movie *The Horse Whisperer*.

"But what I'm very worried about right now," Denise said, "is the stuff inside."

Yeah, that's the hard stuff.

"There's . . . a lot," I said.

"I know." Denise smiled. "I didn't fall off the turnip truck yesterday."

"I don't even know what to say."

"Well, promise me something." Denise's eyes were on the road. "Promise me you'll come back to the farm."

I stared down at the floorboards of the truck, where strands of hay had gathered along with a dirt chunk and a piece of blue baling twine. That was not what I'd expected her to say. She should be yelling at me or pursing her lips and clenching her jaw like Grams did when she was angry. I'd completely messed up, and she wanted me to come back? Places like her farm needed steady people, not hormonal teen girls who couldn't even listen to instructions.

"Is it a deal?" Denise asked.

I swallowed. "Why?"

"Why what?"

"Why do you want me to come back? I screwed things up."

"Shay, that's what our farm's about. Second chances. Strudel's an example. His previous owners gave up on him, but luckily, he ended up here, and we're giving him the best chance to heal from everything he's been through." She pulled up to a stoplight. "Though I will say he does have to work a little bit more on . . . sudden changes of direction."

That brought a smile to my face. "Um, maybe a little bit."

"But you know what? There's grace for him as much as there is for you."

Grace. Now there was a concept I didn't know a lot about, but my heart yearned to understand. This woman was being way nicer than I deserved, but according to her, that was the point.

"Okay," I said softly.

Denise raised her eyebrows at me.

"I'll come back."

Chapter
37

"WELL, AREN'T WE QUITE THE PAIR?"

Aunt Laura and I sat on the couch together, me with a bandaged arm and feeling sore all over, her with a headache and other matching aches and pains.

"Care for some Tylenol?" My aunt rattled the bottle like a maraca.

I laughed. "Oh, stop, please. That hurts."

"I hear ya, kid!"

Stanley jumped up onto the couch and bumped my arm, which also sent pain shooting through my body, and I curled into a ball on the end of the couch. That only made him try to make sure I knew he was there. I covered my face with my hands and felt his long, wet, cold nose nuzzling me.

We'd gotten home from the urgent care facility an hour before. Aunt Laura had borrowed Ginny's car and met us there despite the doctor's warning, and she and Denise had talked while a nurse cleaned my wound and I got stitched up. I couldn't hear what they were saying half the time, and I wasn't sure if that was a good thing or not.

I pulled out my phone. I'd missed a few texts to our group thread.

Tessa: I'm sorry things turned out like that. Please talk to us when you can.

Amelia: Let us know when you're home!

Nothing from Izzy, of course.

I texted back: Home now.

I didn't have the energy for much else. I hoped they'd understand and that we could work things out, but I wasn't sure how I was going to face them again.

"So . . ." Aunt Laura crossed her arms.

"I know, I was stupid."

"That's not exactly what—"

"No, really. I was so dumb." I sat up and tried to get comfortable, but Stanley hadn't left me much room.

"Well, I will say that wasn't your brightest idea."

I sighed in agreement.

"But that Denise lady says she wants you back, so it couldn't have been too bad, right?"

"She did?" I hadn't been sure Denise had meant what she said. I guess she had.

Aunt Laura sighed. "You've had a rough go, kid, but that doesn't give you an excuse for making reckless choices."

"I know."

My aunt reached out for me, and I hesitated, holding my arms around myself. I shook my head a little, not because I didn't want to receive her affection but because I felt entirely unworthy of it. I'd been trying to figure out how to tell my aunt about what I had been doing in secret.

"I did something super bad," I said.

Aunt Laura chuckled. "Can't say running off on a horse was smart."

"Not that."

I rubbed Stanley's ear, unable to look at my aunt. "There's . . . girl stuff I never got to talk to Dad about," I started.

My aunt shifted to her listening position. "Okay."

I wished she could instantly know what I was saying without me having to spell it out. "This is hard to talk about," I said.

"I can see that," Aunt Laura said. "You're not going to shock me, okay? I've made mistakes in my life too."

I swallowed back my fear and kept my eyes on Stanley. This wasn't going to be any easier the longer I put it off. "Like, about sex and things like that."

"Not exactly an easy subject to talk to your dad about."

"No."

"Or me."

I needed to just do this. "I . . . ended up reading some stuff and . . . looking at stuff that I shouldn't have." I risked a glance at my aunt, and instead of surprise or disappointment, I only saw kindness on her face. Her eyes softened, and she reached out for me again. This time I let her pull me into a hug, and I cried on her shoulder without saying another word.

"It's going to be okay," Aunt Laura whispered. "It really is."

After a minute, I pulled back and shared a little more, and she kept a comforting hand on my knee.

"I'm glad you told me. That was very brave of you."

"I don't know what to do." I wiped at my eyes, sniffing back the drippy snot that comes with crying.

"I think you know this is serious, right? It isn't something you just brush away."

I nodded. "I thought it was only a guy thing . . ."

Aunt Laura gently squeezed my shoulder. "No, Shay, it's a human thing. Everyone has their own struggles and temptations.

God created us with sexual desires, and curiosity is normal—for men *and* women. It's what we *do* with temptation that counts. But no, it's not just a guy problem. And you need to know there's nothing wrong with you. You're not dirty or damaged or anything like that."

"I can't believe I even started it. Then I couldn't stop." I felt tears come again. "I was curious . . . and then . . ."

"Pornography is more than pictures, Shay. It can be anything that is meant to cause strong sexual desires. The pictures—or words—can act like a drug," my aunt said. "I don't know the psychology behind it, but a little makes you want more. I think teenagers are especially vulnerable because of their raging hormones. I'm sure we can help you find good, healthy ways to get some of those answers you're looking for."

Something came over me, and I quickly got up from the sofa. For a moment I felt light-headed, but then it cleared. I rushed to my room and pulled the book I'd been reading out from under the bed. A flush of embarrassment warmed my cheeks at the sight of the cover again, but I pushed it away.

I brought the novel to my aunt and reluctantly handed it to her, facedown.

She turned it over, and I saw something zap across her face. Anger?

"This was in the store?" she asked.

I nodded.

"Where?"

"Romance section."

Aunt Laura sighed. "This book should never have been on my shelves." She set the novel on the floor and reached for my hands. She held mine in both of hers, looking up at me. "I'm not sure how it got there, but I'm going to go through every single book in that section and get rid of anything that resembles this."

I nodded again.

"But I need you to do something too, Shay."

"Okay."

"There are going to be temptations. We might miss a book. You might see something on your phone, and curiosity could pull you so hard you feel like you can't resist." Aunt Laura squeezed my fingers. "But I need you to talk to me or someone else if it becomes too much."

"I'll . . . try."

"If you mess up, tell me. If you need help, ask me. Ask Jesus for help too. You aren't alone in this. We all have our own struggles. Your friends, me, your grandmother—we're all trying our best."

"I wish I knew why I did it. Was it because I was so lonely? Or because of what I was learning about my mom?" I said.

"We can talk about that, too, if you want. But we can't let this go on. You get that, right?"

I did. Oh, I did.

"Why couldn't I have just had an ordinary life?" I said, sitting down on the sofa again.

My aunt laughed.

"What?"

"Look at us, Shay." My aunt waved toward the dog, the cat, the apartment. "What's ordinary? All your friends have their stuff to deal with too."

I responded with a small smile.

"But seriously, there's no such thing as ordinary."

Aunt Laura and I sat together for the rest of the evening and watched superhero shows on Netflix. Stanley slept soundly, and at one point I even drifted off too. By the time I made it into my own bed, the second round of Tylenol had alleviated my physical pain, and Aunt Laura had helped with the rest. But there were still two things I had to do.

I pulled up my phone and found Zoe's contact info.

I texted her: Hey, did you mean it when you said we could talk?

Then I pulled up my e-mail account and went to my Drafts folder. I found the e-mail I'd crafted to Mason King. By writing him, I'd been desperately trying to fill the Mom- and Dad-sized holes in my heart. But my "family" had been in front of me all along, hadn't they? My aunt, who really was my blood, but also my friends and *their* families and people like Zoe, who was my sister in Christ. Maybe I had what I needed and didn't need to go down this path just yet. My biological father could wait. Someday I might reconsider, but if I contacted him, it couldn't be to fill a hole. I needed to be okay without him first.

I deleted the e-mail.

Chapter
38

I slept in the next morning, and if it hadn't been for Matilda walking on my head, I probably wouldn't have woken up before noon. I made my way into the kitchen, still dressed in my pajamas. Aunt Laura wasn't around, so I guessed she was already in the bookstore.

At the kitchen table was a note from her, and sitting beside it was my mom's journal. I picked up the lined piece of paper:

Shay,
I'm proud of you. You're one of the smartest, strongest girls
I know. But don't keep trying to do everything by yourself.
We've seen where that gets us!

I read your mom's journal. I see why you found it hard,
but I wanted to make sure you read the last entry. I hope it
helps.

Love,
Aunt Laura

I picked up the leather book and held it in my hands. I hadn't wanted to see this thing again. It was pretty clear how my mom had felt, and that was something I was going to have to deal with. But Aunt Laura wanted me to read the last entry, and I owed her.

She'd marked the last two pages with a blue Post-it Note.

"Okay, here goes," I whispered to Stanley, who lay down in front of me, staring up, hoping for a second breakfast.

The last entry was written with a blue ballpoint pen, and the handwriting seemed firm and decisive, unlike a few of the entries where Mom's trembling hand had caused the lines to stray. I started to read while holding my breath.

> The past few weeks have been awful. My debate wars on inside, and I wake up one morning knowing what I have to do, but by nightfall my resolve fails me. I know, and then I don't. I look at Greg, and my heart aches. He deserves better. I've caused him so much turmoil and pain. He once was happy. I haven't been good to him. I look at little Shay, and my heart cries.

I stopped for a second, took a breath, and tried to go on. Me. She was writing about me.

> She is beautiful beyond anything I could have hoped for. My baby girl. The child I didn't know I needed. How can I damage her by staying? I know what will happen. I know how it will go. She will be better off with Greg and his wonderful, fatherly love. He knows how to love. I do not. Shay deserves more than what I can give her. This is why I know I have to leave. Shay needs much better than me. I will forever love her, but I cannot risk hurting her with who I am.

Aunt Laura found me at the kitchen table, with the book open and my tears falling. She pulled out the other kitchen chair, sat beside me, and made sure I knew I wasn't alone.

—ɯ—

That afternoon I made good on my promise to both my aunt and Denise when I found myself at Second Chance Farm. Denise met me, and we walked over to the horse she knew I'd want to see.

Strudel poked his head over his stall door, ready for treats. I rubbed his neck, glad he didn't seem any worse for wear. I couldn't say the same for myself. I held up my arm to the pony.

"See what you did?"

He took one look and started to nibble the gauze of my bandage with his floppy lips.

"Hey!"

"Silly horse," Denise said.

"Horse? Not a pony?"

The older woman patted Strudel on the top of his head. "Haflingers are actually considered horses, albeit small ones."

"I have a lot to learn," I said.

She smiled. "That you do."

"Hey, sorry I'm late."

I turned around at Tessa's voice. She surprised me by wearing jeans and sneakers; her hair was still damp from swim lessons. We stood there facing each other for a second, and I searched her expression for signs of what she was thinking. She was rarely easy to read. I'd texted her, asking if she'd come, and she'd texted back a simple Sure, okay.

I expected things were going to be very weird. I was probably going to get a friend scolding.

Denise left us alone, and that made the situation even more uncomfortable.

But before I could say a word or guess the meaning behind

her kind, tear-filled eyes, Tessa reached out and hugged me. Not a perfunctory hug like my grandmother sometimes gave me, but the real kind only a friend who loved you could offer.

I'd let her down. I'd been dishonest. I hadn't been a very good friend to her.

And yet . . . here we were.

Tessa held on to me, and I to her, and even though she didn't speak, when she let me go, I felt like she'd spoken a whole library. "I told you I'm not going anywhere," she said softly.

"Me either," another voice said.

I swung around to see Amelia standing right behind me. She'd agreed to meet me here as well. In one fell swoop, she wrapped me up in a hug too, and I gulped air because she squeezed me so hard.

"We want to apologize for being so judgmental," Tessa said gently. "It doesn't help anything to have friends kicking you when you're down."

All I could whisper to both of them was "Thank you."

When Amelia let me go, she gave my good arm a little whack. "And don't scare us like that!"

"Sorry," I said sheepishly.

"I thought you were going to die!" Amelia said with a dramatic flair that didn't seem fake.

"Gonna take more than a horse to do that," I said with a smile.

"I'm glad you're okay," Tessa said.

I cocked my head and looked at her long and hard, determined to be 100 percent truthful. "You know, Tessa, I'm not okay. I really screwed up."

"Yeah," she said, and I wasn't offended she agreed with me. "But we're going to get through this together."

Tessa squeezed my shoulder on one side, and Amelia rested her arm across my back from the other.

"You can't get rid of us that easily," Amelia said.

She said *us*, but I felt Izzy's absence more than I could explain. I knew I'd hurt her deeply, but I'd hoped we could at least start the mending process. I'd sent her several texts in the last day, and it hurt far worse than the cut on my arm that she hadn't responded to any of them.

"She's not coming, is she?" I said, trying not to cry.

"She just needs some time," Tessa said.

I could only hope that was true.

For now, I'd have to be thankful for the two friends who stood by me at this moment. Because of them—and Izzy, too—I felt like I belonged here in Riverbend. They were helping me believe it was okay to be just me: Shay Mitchell, the crazy horse girl. So what if I was motherless and fatherless? I had my aunt, I had the horses, and I had my friends.

Maybe that was enough.

Check out the suspenseful adventures in the High Water™ novel series.

Whether he's facing down alligators in Florida or ghosts in Massachusetts, Parker Buckman keeps finding himself right in the middle of a mystery ... **and danger!**

Join Parker as he risks everything to help his friends and learns to trust in God's perfect timing.

Keep an eye out for more books to come!

Read *Easy Target*, another great novel by Tim Shoemaker!

Taking on bullies comes with hidden danger ... becoming one yourself. Ex-homeschooler Hudson Sutton is thrust into public school his eighth-grade year. He's an outsider—and an easy target. When he sticks up for "Pancake" he makes two allies—and plenty of enemies.

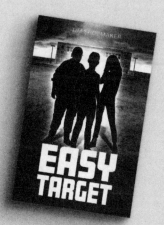

Get these books, and more, at:
FocusOnTheFamily.com/HighWater

FOCUS ON THE FAMILY.

CP1896